"You're Free Enough with Your Kisses," James Said.

With any other man Sarah would have made a joke of it, kissing him on the cheek and laughing as if she hadn't a care in the world. But with this man she could only stare, her eyes dark with a kind of fear she had never felt before.

His lips moved against hers with an unexpected gentleness and she felt a swift rush of pleasure. Too quickly he released her. "It's a pity any man will do," he said coldly. "Because you kiss very nicely, Sarah Gilbert. Practice makes perfect, as they say."

ELIZABETH HUNTER
uses the world as her backdrop. She paints with broad and colorful strokes, yet she is meticulous in her eye for detail. Well known for her warm understanding of her characters, she is internationally beloved by her loyal and enthusiastic readers.

Dear Reader:

I'd like to take this opportunity to thank you for all your support and encouragement of Silhouette Romances.

Many of you write in regularly, telling us what you like best about Silhouette, which authors are your favorites. This is a tremendous help to us as we strive to publish the best contemporary romances possible.

All the romances from Silhouette Books are for you, so enjoy this book and the many stories to come.

Karen Solem
Editor-in-Chief
Silhouette Books

ELIZABETH HUNTER
Pathway to Heaven

Silhouette *Romance*

Published by Silhouette Books New York

America's Publisher of Contemporary Romance

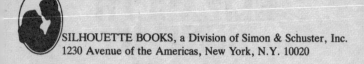

SILHOUETTE BOOKS, a Division of Simon & Schuster, Inc.
1230 Avenue of the Americas, New York, N.Y. 10020

Distributed by Pocket Books

ISBN: 0-671-57322-5

First Silhouette Books printing October, 1984

10 9 8 7 6 5 4 3 2 1

Map by Ray Lundgren

America's Publisher of Contemporary Romance

Printed in the U.S.A.

BC91

Books by Elizabeth Hunter

Silhouette Romance

To Nancy D. Jackson, the best of editors,
because of the letters she writes
and because I like and admire her very much.
A salute from this side of the Atlantic.

Chapter One

Sarah was laughing. She didn't mind the large man's clumsy attempts to kiss her. It was only a bit of fun and she knew it. With practised ease, she avoided being caught in his plump embrace, about to whisper something in his ear. Only, she never did so. Over the man's shoulder she came face to face with someone she was quite sure she had never seen before. Moreover, the stranger was not laughing. The look he was giving her was one of something very like contempt. Perhaps he thought she carried on like this all the time.

"Behave yourself, Richard!"

She lifted his arm and made her escape by the simple expedient of walking underneath it. The stranger was not mollified. He wasn't even English, she thought, at least not judging by his clothes. It was impossible to define quite what the difference was, but it was as clear as daylight. What was he? Australian? American? In Boston, England, he was bound to be one or the other—unless he was Dutch, and she didn't think he was that. She was as sure that he wasn't a European at all.

"Can I help you?" she asked him.

"I doubt it."

Sarah felt herself flush. "Richard and I have just discovered we're related," she explained.

"Kissing cousins?" the man asked.

American, she decided, and sighed. "I should have thought that was obvious," she returned. She opened her decidedly green eyes wide and favoured him with a bland stare that wouldn't have fooled anyone who knew her well. "Jealous?" she challenged.

The American shrugged his shoulders. He wasn't as tall as Richard, but he was in far better condition, she noted.

"Not at all. When I kiss someone I like to have their full attention."

She sucked in her lower lip, amused despite herself. "Let me guess," she murmured. "You're from Boston, Massachusetts, and you're over here looking up your ancestors."

For the first time the American looked less than confident. "It wasn't my idea."

"What name are you looking for?"

"Bradstreet."

"Well, that's easy, Mr. Bradstreet. Simon Bradstreet, son-in-law of Thomas Dudley and his successor in office, was steward and governor of Massachusetts from 1679 to 1686 and from 1689 to 1692."

"I happen to know that, Miss—Miss . . ."

"Gilbert. Sarah Gilbert."

"Is that a local name?"

"It certainly is! We didn't go to America, however. My ancestor served as astronomer on Cook's second expedition. Our connections with Australia are even closer in some ways than they are with your city."

"Really?"

Sarah's temper flared. "Ever heard of Banks, Bass, Franklin and Flinders?" she demanded.

"I guess so."

"Well, they all came from round here. There's a plaque in the church under the church tower in their memory." She shut her eyes and quoted from heart, " 'In proud memory of George Bass, Surgeon once of this town and of others who lived nearby and with him bore a gallant part in the exploration of Australia.' My ancestor Joseph Gilbert is on that plaque."

"Is that what brought you into the business of tracing other peoples' ancestors?"

"Mmm. 'These were honoured in their generation and were the glory of their times . . .' "

Richard came suddenly back to life. "We were drinking champagne when you came in. Sit down, Mr. American, and help us finish the bottle."

"Bradstreet," Sarah prompted him.

The American sat on one of the solid carved oak chairs Sarah kept in her office. He managed to make it look quite fragile, something that Richard's mountainous bulk had never been able to do. Whatever else this American was, he was all man. Sarah could feel the strength of his masculinity clear across the room. It made her flesh tingle in a way that was really rather pleasant. She wondered what he'd say if he knew that his mere presence in the room was having more effect on her than Richard's close embrace. She turned to look at him, a hint of speculation in her eyes, and found he was already looking her up and down in a way that gave her a funny feeling in her middle.

"Bradstreet is my mother's name," he said, more to Richard than to her. "It's because of her that I'm here."

"Don't look at me!" Richard backed off. "I've just been through the mill and I know no more about it than when I started."

Sarah winced. "Richard wanted to prove his entitlement to put in a claim on a local estate. He's what used to be known as a gentleman farmer, and he wants to get his hands on the land next to his, which happens to be entailed within a certain family. We were able to prove that he's the most likely male descendant to benefit."

"Don't females count?"

"Only as also-rans. We get used to it, seeing our younger brothers take precedence over us."

The American made a discovery. "You don't care, do you?" He smiled, and it was a fascinating experience to see the amusement crease up his face. He was a handsome devil, she thought, if you liked the macho kind of man.

"Not a lot." She smiled back at him. "I'll get where I'm going through my own efforts, or not at all."

He held out his hand to her. "You'll do, Sarah Gilbert. I'm James Foxe, with an *e*."

That rang a bell. There had been a John Foxe in the sixteenth century, who'd been born in Boston, England, though for the life of her Sarah couldn't remember the details of his story offhand. A familiar sense of excitement gripped her. This was going to be an interesting family tree! She could smell it. She had an instinct for these things that very seldom let her down.

"Welcome to Boston, Lincolnshire," She grinned at him. "I don't think we'll have any trouble finding out who you are."

He looked her straight in the eyes. "I know who I am," he said. "I found that out a long time ago. I don't care a rap who my ancestors are. Unfortunately, my mother does. She got the bug last year and won't be satisfied until everyone is traced back to Adam and Eve."

"We might not be able to go that far back," Sarah interrupted him.

Richard looked at her with very much the same look he'd had just before he'd kissed her. "If anyone can, you can," he declared. "A miracle worker!"

Sarah knew she was nothing of the kind. She put her faith in persistent hard work, getting her results mainly by knowing where to look. Also, she was a good listener and people willingly rehearsed to her every detail they could remember of the stories that had been handed down to them by older members of their families. However, it didn't look as if Mr. Foxe was going to be much help in that respect.

"Hadn't you better be going, Richard?" she suggested smoothly. She had long ago learned that an irritated client could seldom be brought to the point and Richard was doing his best to irritate the American. Stuck-in-the-mud people were apt to look down on anyone whose ancestors had had the courage to cross the seas to make a new life for themselves. She was the product of both types, and she was glad that one side of her family had stayed behind and were still living on the land that had bred their ancestors since the times of Hereward the Wake. Still, she couldn't help preferring the spirit that had taken the other side of her family all over the Commonwealth, taming the wilderness with nothing but bare hands and love for the open space and the freedom they found there.

Richard lumbered to his feet. "Off with the old, on with the new," he grumbled. "I suppose you'll have no more time for me now?"

"I always make time for my friends," Sarah assured him.

"And am I one?"

Sarah squinted up at him with a provocative look. "I don't know, are you?"

"I certainly am! Moreover, you know all about me! What d'you know about this other fellow?" He winked at the American to show him that no offence was intended. It was hard, therefore, that the unknown Mr. Foxe showed every sign of losing his temper.

"Enough," said Sarah. "Go, Richard!"

As the American watched, the big man departed. With a sardonic air he said, "I hope you mean to be as affectionate with me if you're successful in tracing my family tree."

A shock wave passed through Sarah. Was that it? Surely he couldn't have been objecting to Richard's proprietory attitude towards herself, could he? Richard was like some huge mastiff going through the motions of marking out his territory, but no way was he ever going to be top-drawer material for her. One word from her and he would be back on his heels begging for mercy.

"You'll have to wait and see," she said aloud.

"I'm not noted for my patience," he retorted, sitting down on the vacated chair.

She chose to misunderstand him. "In my line of business one has to learn patience, often the hard way." She sat back in her chair, eyeing him warily from beneath her lashes. "'I give you the end of a golden string; Only wind it into a ball, It will lead you in at heaven's gate, Built in Jerusalem's wall.'"

The American's eyes glinted. "Right, Miss Gilbert, you're on! What kind of heaven are you offering me?"

She looked away. "Something rather less than the Garden of Eden, I'm afraid," she murmured.

"The Garden of Eden was always too platonic for my taste," he remarked. "I prefer the time *after* the eating of the fruit of the Tree of Knowledge. How about you?"

"I've never given it any thought," Sarah assured him hastily.

He looked her over in a way that made her long to adjust her blouse in case it was more revealing than she had intended when she put it on in the morning.

"Do you read much Blake, Miss Gilbert?"

"No," she said. Blast the man! She'd been about to fall into the same trap as Richard and think it was only the English who ever read anything. She groaned inwardly. She had a nasty suspicion this man could buy and sell her in any literary competition, and she wished she'd kept her big mouth shut. She hadn't even known it was Blake she had been quoting.

"I thought not," he said dryly.

Sarah strove to remember the rest of the poem, but the only Blake that came to mind was "Tiger, Tiger, burning bright" and the thing called Jerusalem that the Women's Institutes sang at all their meetings.

"I was merely trying to point out the excitement of the chase," she said, primping up her mouth because she suspected he was going to laugh at the excuse, one she didn't think much of herself.

"Ah, now that is something you might know about!" he mocked. "Or is Big Richard the only swain of the moment?"

She glared across the desk. "Is that any of your business?"

"I just wondered how many others had been offered a taste of that heaven of yours?"

She sat up very straight, taking a deep breath to steady her nerves. "You can't expect heaven in this world, Mr. Foxe. Concentrate on the golden string which will unite you with your ancestors at the proper time. All I can do is tell you who they all were."

He grinned, and she thought again how good-looking he was. There was a crease in his left cheek when he smiled which gave his face an asymmetrical look that pleased her. He looked as though he lived hard and played hard—there wasn't an ounce of spare flesh on him. And he had that young, clean look that so many Americans seem to keep into late middle age. It made it difficult for her to tell his age, but she guessed him to be in his late twenties or early thirties. Often one could tell a person's age by their hands, but his hands were as superbly kept as the rest of him. There was also a tang of after-shave that would set him apart from most of his English counterparts. She liked it. She liked too his neatly brushed hair that was busily escaping the discipline he imposed on it. It had a life of its own, standing on end no matter what he did to it.

"It'll do—as a beginning! Where do we start?"

With difficulty, Sarah brought her concentration back to the subject of genealogy. She sorted the papers in front of her, pushing them away into drawers with an arbitrary hand. It would be her own fault if she couldn't find anything after this! She cleared her throat and smiled a would-be professional smile at her tormentor.

"If your mother has been interested in tracing her family for a year or more, I suppose she's done most of the American side. Has she any record of when any of them crossed the Atlantic?"

James Foxe reached into his pocket and produced a wad of papers. "Some of them went with the Arbella—"

"That's a good beginning! Most of the people who went on the Arbella came from Boston."

"But not John Foxe?"

"Well, no, he was earlier than that." Sarah had succeeded in placing John Foxe by now. "He died in 1587, nearly two years before John Cotton, Vicar of both Boston, Lincolnshire, and Boston, Massachusetts, was born. It was Cotton's preaching that led to so many of Boston's citizens' crossing the Atlantic and founding New Boston over there."

"According to Mother, Cotton's eldest son Seaborn

married a Dorothy Bradstreet. He was in the ministry at Hampton, New Hampshire."

"Well, that's a start," Sarah encouraged him. "You seem to be connected to a lot of famous people. That makes it much easier!"

"Tell me about John Foxe," he said.

"He was born in Boston. He wrote the Book of Martyrs. You can see a copy in the Guild Hall Museum and there's another one in the library of St. Botolph's Church—"

"The Boston Stump?"

"That's what we all call it."

"Why?"

She shrugged her shoulders. "Who knows? It may be because you see it for miles round, across the fens; or because it was once meant to have a steeple on the top of the lantern tower; or that it was seventy years in the building and people gave up hope of its ever being finished."

"There must be quite a view from the top," he ventured.

"There is, if you can manage the three hundred and sixty-five steps to the top. One for every day of the year."

"I think I might manage that. I'm in pretty good shape. How about you?"

"Now?" she demanded, appalled.

His smile grew broader, dazzling her into accepting anything he suggested. "I'll give you lunch afterwards," he offered.

She put his mother's papers to one side and stood up, smiling also. "Okay," she said. "I'll show you the Cotton Chapel on the way, if we can get past the builders. It's mostly financed with American money. You may as well see what your dollars are doing for the town."

He held her coat for her with an ease and grace that she hadn't met with often in the men she knew.

"Don't you approve, Miss Gilbert?"

"Not entirely. We live here and you don't. It's nice to have the connection, but we ought to maintain our own monuments instead of forever holding out our hands and waiting for the Almighty Dollar to fall into it. You Americans are such suckers when it comes to a bit of history!"

"That comes well from someone in your profession," he answered soberly. "What else do you do, Miss Gilbert?"

"I try to give value for money. I put in as much as I take out . . ."

He was amused. "I see that not all the Puritans came across to our Boston."

"My ancestors went to Australia," she reminded him proudly. "And none of them were Puritans, so far as I know."

"I see, it just rubbed off on you along the way?"

"It did not! It just irritates me that anyone in need of any money runs off to America to raise it over there. It's our history too!"

"Don't we get any good marks for generosity?" he enquired meekly.

She turned and looked at him. "Is that what you want?"

He shook his head. "Not me, Miss Gilbert. I look at every cent twice before I spend it. You won't be making your fortune out of me."

She wondered if he were joking, and decided he was not. He looked completely serious, almost grim. He must be fond of his mother to go to all this trouble to indulge her whim, she thought.

She thanked him for his help with her coat, picking up her bag from under her desk. "I resect people who know the value of money," she began almost timidly. She hadn't meant to sound critical of Americans—it was the English Bostonians who took the dollars as if it were their right . . .

"If you're expecting me to fight you over your fee, you'll be disappointed. I'm far too frightened of going back home to my mother without the information she wants."

Sarah didn't believe a word of it. She looked suitably humble. "I charge a lot, but I'm worth it. I've never had a disappointed client yet."

"Male or female?"

Sarah looked down her nose. "I don't dis- criminate—"

"You kiss us all with equal fervour?"

"Oh, that! Richard easily gets excited about noth- ing at all. It doesn't mean anything."

"It meant something to him."

Sarah had been worried about that too, but she couldn't see what she could do about it. Richard was Richard, and there was little harm in his kissing her, after all.

"Tough," she said out loud.

"Heartless wench. When I kiss you, you won't get away with shrugging me off like that."

Sarah already knew that. She preceded him out of the office, locking the door carefully behind her.

"I may not kiss you at all," she said. "I don't suppose we're related or connected in any way."

He put up a hand and gave a gentle tug to the knot at the nape of her neck where she had wound up her long, blonde hair to get it out of her way.

"I'm holding tight to the end of the golden string. Isn't that how I find the gate to heaven?"

Sarah was winded. She gasped for breath and hoped he wouldn't notice. She would need all her wits to deal with this man, and she wasn't quite sure she wanted to. It was a strange temptation, one she had never met with before, to lean back against him and let him take over. He probably didn't mean to kiss her at all, but he'd managed to get the idea so firmly embedded in her mind that it was difficult to think of anything else. Of one thing she was quite sure: it would be a very different thing from being kissed by Richard, or any of the other men who had asked her out and flirted with her a little until she had called the whole thing off. She had a nasty suspicion that it wouldn't be she who would be in control of any relationship she might have with James Foxe. And that wasn't the way she played, so what was she going to do?

She turned her head to find her hair was still held in the palm of his hand. "Please let me go!"

"You only had to ask," he said.

She wasn't used to asking. She thought of telling him so, but then thought better of it.

She walked in front of him along the corridor and down the narrow flight of stairs that led straight out into the street. She wouldn't think about him at all—that was the answer! But it didn't work—all the time she could feel his eyes boring into her back. Was her skirt on straight? Had she smoothed down the collar of her jacket at the back, or left it flying as she sometimes did, the washing instructions sticking out beneath her hair? She kept her hands to her sides, allowing her bag to swing jauntily from the strap over her shoulder. It wasn't very comfortable, but it'd be the last straw if he were to guess how nervous she felt at that moment.

She led the way in silence to the church, crossing the wide marketplace without a backward look. On the right was a pedestrian precinct, and on the left was the road that led down to the Guild Hall, where the first of the Pilgrim Fathers had once been imprisoned for trying to escape to Holland. She thought of pointing it out to him, but she felt safer when they weren't talking. She'd take him there afterwards and do it properly, she promised silently. She'd have got her nerve back by then. Great Scot, she was re-nowned in her family for having the last word on any and every subject. Surely, her ready tongue wasn't going to fail her now, was it?

Their tour of the church was sedate. Sarah showed him everything she thought he ought to see, ignoring his cool indifference to the monuments that had been put up to his ancestors. Sarah tried to sound enthusi-astic, but the only moment she was sincerely moved was when she showed him the tablet the Australians had put up to commemorate their own founders.

"There's *my* ancestor!"

"So I see," he said.

She ground her teeth. "It's interesting to me!" she claimed.

"You and my mother would make a fine pair," he said. "She takes credit for everything her ancestors did too."

Sarah faced him. "Why not?"

"Aren't you afraid of finding any skeletons in your cupboard?" he mocked her.

She shook her head. "Why should I?"

"They have a way of falling out on one when they're least welcome," he told her.

"How would you know?" she demanded.

"A lawyer sees more than most of the seamy side of humanity."

She hadn't known he was a lawyer. She thought of Perry Mason and wondered if he defended people with the same flair. Perhaps he had enough interest in his life not to need his ancestors to boost his ego.

"You'd better see the Cotton Chapel before we go up the tower," she said. She was looking forward to telling him all about the chapel.

"Renovated with American money?" he asked from the doorway.

"Of course." She warmed to the task ahead of her. It was a pity the builders were still working inside, spoiling the full effect. "It may have started out as the burial place of Dame Margaret Tilney, who laid the foundation stone of the tower. Later it was a Charity School and then it housed the town's fire engine. In 1857 it was restored under the direction of Gilbert Scott—"

"Liverpool Cathedral?"

"Yes," she agreed. She couldn't stop smiling over the next bit. "He wanted to paint the roof with stars and stripes."

"But somebody's better sense prevailed?" he groaned.

She nodded, laughing. "The vicar's. He said it was too popish!"

"You're not serious?"

She nodded again, enjoying herself. "I am!"

He ran a finger down the bridge of her nose, smiling straight into her eyes. She felt completely at home with him in that moment. They understood one another, not at a level that she could have explained if anyone had asked her about it, but they weren't strangers any longer. With any luck, she thought, she'd made a friend.

"Are you ready to climb the tower?" she asked.

She had been up the tower several times before, of course, so she knew how the wind buffeted the two-hundred-foot-high structure. The doors that opened to the newel stairs were eighteenth-century Gothic and, during the lower part of the climb, small blocked windows showed that the turret was part of the old west front that was in place from before the time the tower was built. Iron collars and reinforced concrete floors to the galleries helped to bind the tower together. In a high wind, Sarah knew from experience, they seemed totally inadequate, yet they had survived four centuries and would probably survive as many more. Bostonians wouldn't like it at all if their famous Boston Stump were to crumble and fall down.

The first balcony gave the best view of the town.

Sarah pointed out the docks to the south, the Wash and sometimes the distant Norfolk coast to the east, and to the north the Grand Sluice, Tattershall Castle and, if one was very lucky, Lincoln Cathedral standing more than forty miles away.

"I forgot to show you the pulpit," Sarah said on the way down. "John Cotton was the first to use it. He would often preach for two or three hours at a time."

"It seems to me you were well rid of him," Mr. Foxe responded.

Sarah flashed him a sunny smile. "He talked a great many citizens into leaving before he went himself. He was too ill of an ague, which carried off his first wife. He married again, of course." She screwed up her nose. "I must say, I think you were welcome to him."

The American opened the doors for her at the foot of the stairs and somehow managed to take her hand in his in the process, pulling her back to face him.

"What happened to the old man in the end?" he asked.

Sarah opened her eyes very wide. "He crossed the ferry at Boston to preach in Cambridge and he caught a cold and died."

"Serves him right!" James Foxe declared with feeling. "Now, where can we eat? I'm starving, even if you're not."

Chapter Two

Sarah nearly dropped the guitar she was carrying as James Foxe fell into step beside her.

"I thought you'd gone back to London." she said.

He took the guitar from her, looking pleased with himself. "I decided to stay on for a while. Where are you off to?"

Sarah recovered herself with difficulty, more than a little dismayed by the warm trickle of pleasure that was spreading through her body. It was ridiculous to be quite so pleased to see him. It was even more ridiculous to stand in the middle of the pavement like a looney, hardly able to remember just where it was that she was going.

"A group of us get together every Tuesday night to play and sing. We're not much good, but we're madly keen."

"Mind if I come along?"

Sarah gave him a startled glance. "You won't enjoy it! Most of the songs we murder are American in origin—"

"As long as it won't cost me anything." He cut her off without a glimmer of a smile.

Sarah thought what a feather in her cap it would be to arrive with an American lawyer from Boston, Massachusetts, in tow, and almost rubbed her hands in glee. They would have welcomed him anyway, but James Foxe was more than presentable—he was positively dishy, and she defied anyone to say otherwise.

"It might cost you a song," she warned him.

"I'll write one for you to sing."

She looked at him again, seeking to read what was in his mind, but his face gave nothing away. "Can you?" she asked him doubtfully.

"Wait and see!"

It was only when she opened the door to the church hall that she wondered what Paul would think of her new escort. Paul and she weren't exactly in love and they never had been, but they went about together when it was convenient for them both. Sarah had thought at one time that their relationship might grow into something warmer, but it never had. Occasionally they kissed, and that was nice, they both enjoyed it, but neither of them had ever caught fire and wanted more.

Paul was a dear, but men were peculiar beings and, even though he didn't want her for himself, he could well turn nasty when she turned up with somebody else. Look at the way Richard had behaved! And he had far less cause than Paul to think somebody might trespass on his preserves.

She held out her hand for her guitar. "Listen, everybody, this is James Foxe from Boston, America. He's come to hear us sing."

The group of friends clustered about him, all of them laughing and talking together, asking him questions that Sarah wouldn't have asked them after weeks of getting to know them. They wanted to know his age, the name of his girl friend—or was it his wife?—and she found herself listening intently, as if the answers really mattered to her. He was thirty-two and he had never married, though he had come close to it once or twice.

"I want something more than 'we may as well,'" he told them frankly. "I shan't marry until I can't imagine living without the girl."

Paul turned his back on the proceedings. "He'll be lucky!" he said with a bitterness that surprised Sarah. "Most of us have to compromise in the end. What makes him think he'll find the perfect mate?"

"I think he might," said Sarah.

Paul put a hand on her shoulder. "You made a mistake bringing him here," he told her. "He'll take over. His sort always do!"

"I like him," Sarah maintained.

"You never did have any sense when it came to men!" Paul snorted. "It's a good thing you have me to look after you."

Sarah was less than convinced. She was even more doubtful when he put his other arm over her other shoulder and pulled her up hard against him, kissing her deliberately on the mouth. She knew without even looking that he had timed his embrace for that moment because James Foxe was looking their way.

Yet it would have been unkind not to have kissed him back. She and Paul were known as a couple, and it would have caused a lot of gossip if she had pulled away and told him to leave her alone. Their friends were bound to think it was because she had come in with James. They might even jump to the conclusion that it was the American she wanted to go home with afterwards! That was a thought to bring her up with a jolt. She wasn't ready to be linked with anyone other than Paul.

Satisfied, Paul let her go, giving her a last pat on her behind, which annoyed her far more than the kiss had done. Why couldn't he keep his hands to himself?

"What are you going to sing?" he asked her.

She took her guitar out of its case and strummed a few notes on it. "I haven't got anything new." She thought about it for a moment. There wasn't much point in singing anything if everyone was going on talking to James all evening. Then she opened her mouth, knowing she was about to annoy Mr. Foxe. 'Yankee Doodle came to town, riding on a pony; stuck a feather in his cap, and called it macaroni.'

James Foxe raised his brows in a mocking glance. "One of ours, Miss Gilbert? I should've thought you had enough songs of your own?"

She wished she hadn't tried to get a rise out of him. "We sing American songs all the time," she muttered.

"What about American-style dancing?"

"That too," she admitted reluctantly.

He took her guitar from her and walked away to one end of the hall, tapping his foot on the floor to get the right rhythm. She didn't know what she'd expected, but it certainly was not the breathless barn dance that followed. He had them all bobbing and swinging from side to side in response to the nonstop nonsense that came out of his mouth. But it nevertheless kept them going, interpreting the dance as they went on. It wasn't Sir Roger de Coverley; it was better. Or he was the most brilliant caller she had ever heard, and that didn't seem likely, not in a lawyer from New England.

Sarah enjoyed dancing, and she had never been known to be short of partners. She went happily from man to man, only half aware of Paul glowering at her on the sidelines. Paul danced as if he had two left feet, and was apt to sulk if he didn't get his own way. Too bad, she thought; let him get on with it! It was only half an hour later that she remembered him again and took pity on him, restraining her own exuberance long enough to pause beside him and sympathise with him. He didn't much enjoy coming to hear her sing, and yet he always did, week after week, to please her.

"You'd find it fun if you'd let yourself go!" she told him.

"Would I?"

"*I* do!"

Paul glared at her. "I care whom I'm dancing with! You'd let any man swing you about and trample on your toes!"

"Most of them don't do that," she denied. She ought to be laughing, she thought, but all she felt was bleak inside. If Paul got serious about her she would be losing a friend, one that she'd valued more than most, and her friends were the most important thing in her life.

"Would you care if they did as long as they're

paying you the court and telling you you're beautiful?"

She tried to turn that into a joke. "Am I beautiful,
Paul?"

"Ask that American chap you came with."

She straightened her back. "He's a guest in our
country—"

"I didn't invite him and neither did you!"

"That's beside the point. I'm working for him. His
people came from Boston in the first place. He's
almost one of us."

"If that's all he means to you, come home with me
now and we can listen to some real music instead of
having to put up with this din."

Sarah had forgotten for the moment that he didn't
like any pop music. She'd put it at the back of her
mind because she'd thought it ridiculous to brand
anything but the classics as being for the simple-
minded. She never wanted to think badly of people
and she seldom dwelt on their weaknesses. She resented having this one brought forcibly into view at
this particular moment.

"I'm enjoying myself here," she said.

"And you don't care that I'm not?"

She had never quarrelled with Paul in all the years
she'd known him. She looked him straight in the eye
and said, "Not particularly. You're not the only
pebble on the beach. You could try to have a good
time so as not to spoil it for everyone else."

Paul stuck an angry finger in her face. "You'd like
that, wouldn't you? I don't need everybody's approval for everything I do—not even yours! If you won't
come with me, I'll go alone!"

Sarah turned her back on him, allowing the next man who came along to reclaim her for the dance. Tomorrow, she would soothe Paul's ruffled feathers and bring him out of his sulk, but tonight she couldn't resist making the most of the impromptu dance. Paul would be upset that she hadn't gone with him, but he'd get over it. They nearly always did what he wanted when they went out together; surely it was only fair that she should dance the night away on the one evening of the week she kept for her hobby. She had never asked him to come along and listen to their group, though she had to admit she had been flattered that he did come, hardly ever missing one of their performances. Was she being selfish when she knew how he hated making a fool of himself—which he did whenever he tried to dance or sing?

She lost her place in the dance, excused herself, and searched for Paul with her eyes, meaning to go over to him and apologise. She wasn't entirely sorry to see that he was already gone. It might make things more difficult on the morrow, but it meant she had the rest of tonight to herself and that, she assured herself, was the only reason that for the moment it was a relief to be rid of him. Only once in the whole evening did she dance with James Foxe. Someone else had volunteered to do a stint at the piano to relieve him from his self-appointed task as master of ceremonies. A waltz was thumped out on the aging piano and they had danced to it with a sedate formality that was lovely in contrast to the hectic bustle of the dances that had gone before.

"You remind me of a butterfly," James said suddenly. "You flit about the room with all eyes on you, but nobody quite catches hold of you. Why are you so elusive?"

"Am I?"

"Not even your boyfriend seems to have your full attention. Is that why he left?"

She shook her head. "He doesn't like your style of music."

He put his arm closer about her. "Why take it out on you?"

She pulled away. "I get bored listening to his chamber music. I can't tell Amadeus from Mozart. Besides, I *like* dancing, even if he doesn't!"

James Foxe had somehow managed to get closer to her again. "Amadeus was Mozart's middle name."

Her mouth turned up at the corners. "You can try all you like to provoke me, but you won't succeed, you know. Better men than you have tried tonight!"

He laughed out loud. "That's two down," he said. "How many more of them are there to go?"

Sarah thought that a dangerous subject. If she pretended she didn't understand him he might jump to the conclusion that all English women were slow in the uptake. On the other hand . . .

"Why don't you hang around and see?" she invited him.

"Thank you. I will," he replied promptly. "At least for the next fortnight. Will you have dinner with me tomorrow?"

She found herself looking at his mouth rather than his eyes and caught herself up before her imagination ran away with her.

"I'm seeing Paul tomorrow night."

"Thursday?"

She shook her head.

"Friday?"

"I'm going to my mother's for the weekend. You could come with me, I suppose, and see a bit more of the countryside, but her house is small—"

"I'll bring my sleeping bag." He clinched the invitation. "Is your mother anything like you?"

She was dismayed by how easily she had been manipulated into taking him home with her. Her mother was the old-fashioned kind, with the manners of a former age. Sarah only hoped she wouldn't read anything into her bringing a man home. She would have to telephone her and explain she was being kind to a stranger to their shores and hadn't fallen madly in love with him. That wouldn't stop her mother from adding two and two together and making five, but it might stop her putting James through the kind of inquisition that only the well-bred English country lady has the nerve to impose on a completely strange young man. Sarah shuddered at the thought of the inevitable questions. And how many dollars do you earn in a year, Mr. Foxe? Really? What is that in pounds?

"You're looking a bit green round the gills," James Foxe broke into her unwelcome thoughts. "Shall I walk you home?"

"No." She came back to the present with a bang. "No, of course not! You'll want to get back to wherever it is you're staying. I haven't far to go."

"Nevertheless," he said, "I'd prefer to see you safely to your door."

She had an idea that Americans thought such

attentions more important than English men did. She didn't have to ask him in if she didn't want to. She'd explain to him that the sooner she rang her mother and told her she was bringing a guest home for the weekend the better. That sounded reasonable enough, even to her.

It was a lovely night outside. There was a new moon rising over the Stump and Sarah stopped and bowed to it solemnly, turning the loose coins over in her pocket. None of them was real silver and none of them was an old-fashioned sixpenny piece that had used to bring one good luck.

"Last month I saw the new moon through glass," she volunteered by way of explanation at her small charade. "That's supposed to be very unlucky, and it wasn't much of a month. This time I'm taking every precaution."

"Don't you believe in making your own luck?"

"Well, yes. If you believe hard enough in the old superstitions, though, they sometimes come true. I may be making myself a lucky month by mind over matter." She flashed him a smile. "I wouldn't expect a lawyer to believe in such nonsense, so don't look so worried!" she said.

"I want to know why you do."

She didn't think he'd understand. "Someone has to keep up the old traditions," she said. "The machines are taking over. Who believes in the man in the moon any longer?"

"I suppose you blame us for that too!"

"No," she said. She was amused that he should be taking their conversation so seriously. " 'The Man in the Moon may wear out his shoon, by running after Charles-his-Wain. But all's to no end; for the times will not mend, till the King enjoys his own again.'"

"Shoon?"

"His shoes, you loon. We're very close to East Anglia here and they often form a plural with an *n* at the end."

James Foxe looked more confused than ever. "Are you trying to get at me about the king coming into his own again?"

She gave him a cheeky grin. "We-ell," she said, "the Australians remained British, why couldn't you?"

"We called our land New England . . ."

They had reached the house where she lived. She put a hand on his sleeve to point out the way to her door.

"Did you know the queen and George Washington are related?"

To get to her front door they had to walk down a narrow passageway between two ancient stone houses. James held out his hand for her key, opening the door for her and going in first to turn on the light.

"D'you think she knows that?"

"I'm sure somebody will have told her." She held out her hand for her key. "Did I ask you in for coffee, or anything?"

He put the key in the palm of her hand. It was still warm from his touch. "Anything," he decided with a firmness that made her ears burn.

She licked her lips. "I've changed my mind if I did," she said quickly. "I need to warn my mother I'm bringing you with me at the weekend."

"I can wait," he said.

"Not in my place, you can't!"

His eyes were dark and mysterious. She wondered what he'd say if she told him she wasn't sure she wanted him to go either. They hadn't known each other long enough to know if they liked each other or not, but she thought she could like him very much indeed.

"All right," he said. "I'll see you in the morning?"

She looked at him, aghast. "I won't have anything ready for you by then!" she protested.

"I thought I might do some of the work myself—you'll come cheaper if I do." He sounded unbearably cheerful. "Where d'you want your guitar?"

"Anywhere."

He put it carefully up against the wall, then walked right over to where she was standing, crowding her more than a little. But she wouldn't step back—that would be another battle she would have lost.

"I'll say good night," he said. "I've enjoyed the evening."

He was going to kiss her! "You're welcome," she forced out, in conscious imitation of the way she had heard Americans speak in films.

"Good night," he said.

And then he was gone, and he hadn't kissed her at all. He hadn't touched her! He hadn't even smiled at her! She told herself she was glad he had taken her at her word and that if he had kissed her, she certainly wouldn't have kissed him back.

He had a nice mouth, though, and she liked the way he laughed. Paul never really laughed at all. Which reminded her how little she was looking forward to the following evening and bringing Paul out of his annoyance with her. She *liked* Paul, she always had, but her mother didn't like him, and groaned openly when she took him home with her. What would she think of James?

Her mother was a long time answering the phone. "I was just going to give up. I thought you'd gone out," Sarah told her.

"I'd gone to bed."

Sarah wondered what the time was. Judging by her mother's tone, it was late. There was a lengthy silence. "Not asleep, I hope?"

Her mother managed to sound as apologetic as Sarah had. "Not exactly. David had other things on his mind."

Sarah's vision of her stepfather was hardly that of the Great Lover and she was startled to find that her mother probably saw him quite differently. It was a pleasant surprise, on the whole. She'd been glad when her mother had married again soon' after her own father's untimely death. Her mother needed to be married. If she had no husband in the background, what other excuse would she have for dodging all those social chores that were the more boring side of her chosen lifestyle?

"Oh," said Sarah. "I rang to tell you I'm bringing an American home with me next weekend. He says he'll bring his sleeping bag if you're short of beds."

Her mother came immediately to life. "But, darling, that's marvelous! Tell me more."

"There's nothing to tell. I'm researching his family tree—"

"Of course! Is he good-looking?"

Sarah sighed. "He gets by. Look, Mother, I know nothing about him except that he's a lawyer from Boston, U.S.A. I'm not sure if I like him or not. I have no details on his income. He doesn't care who his ancestors were, but his mother does. He seems fond of her."

"He sounds *most* interesting! I'll look forward to meeting him."

Sarah tried again. "Mother, don't read anything into this. He's at a loose end in a foreign country, nothing more than that."

Her mother's voice deepened into a conspiratorial whisper. "I'll be terribly discreet, and David will be, too. Shall I tell Alan and Simon to stay away?"

"Alan and Simon are friends of mine. I'm always pleased to see them," Sarah said, miffed.

"Well, dear, it's your decision, but, if you don't mind my saying so, you can be as clumsy as your father was when it comes to man management. Alan and Simon have got used to sparring with each other over you; your American may not be quite so understanding."

"That's all you know!" Sarah retorted.

"Doesn't he care?" Her mother sounded outraged.

"Mother, I told you, our relationship is professional, and we only met yesterday."

"But you were out with him tonight? Why else are you so late home?"

"He was there," Sarah admitted. "You know I go and sing with the group every Tuesday."

"And he just happened along?"

"I met him along the way and he carried my guitar for me."

"Ah! Perhaps you're managing better than I thought. As long as you keep Paul well out of the way—"

"Mother! James Foxe is thirty-two years old and is in England for two weeks. I've known Paul for years and I'm very fond of him. There's no comparison between them."

"I'm glad to hear it!" her mother answered, and hung up as soon as she'd wished her daughter good night.

Sarah frowned at the burring receiver. Whatever had induced her to invite the American home, anyway? It was going to be a ghastly weekend and there was nothing she could do about it now.

Sarah made herself a hot drink on the gas ring that was built into one corner of her room. When the kettle had boiled and she'd poured it on top of the frothing chocolate, she was tempted to pour it straight down the sink. What she needed was something stronger, some of the hard stuff to steady her nerves. Then she laughed at herself for being ridiculous. It was hardly the end of the world if her mother should be in one of her matchmaking moods all weekend long. Nothing very dreadful could happen in the space of two days, especially if she were to warn James about her mother's obsession. She could drop it into the conversation as she drove him through the fens into Cambridgeshire, where her mother was now living.

She decided to drink the hot chocolate after all. She had never felt less like going to sleep, and she refused to spend the small hours of the morning in a fret about what her mother might or might not say to James

Foxe. Drat the man! He meant nothing to her, so why should she care? The rub was that she did. What had he said when Paul had walked out on the dance? Two down and how many more to go? What would he think of Alan and Simon? Would he understand they were like brothers to her, that she had gone to school with their sisters, and that they only flirted with her now because it had become a habit from the days when they'd first tried impressing her with their newly discovered manhood? And she had used them in the same way, finding her feet in what was a brand new world to her, where she had to stand and wait and they had to find her a chair and carry her things around for her. She had felt as powerful as Queen Cleopatra, or the Empress Catherine. She thought she had learned her lessons well. It was only her mother who thought her clumsy when it came to men.

She finished her chocolate and went to bed, but unfortunately not to sleep. James Foxe had a lot to answer for, she thought with venom as she dressed for work the following day. Would he be at her office again today? Her spirits rose and she was singing under her breath as she hurried through the pedestrian precinct towards her office.

Chapter Three

Sarah's car had seen better days. Her stepfather had presented her with it the day he had married her mother, explaining the unusual reversal of the usual procedure by telling her that she was to visit her mother as often as possible. Else his new wife might regret becoming Mrs. David Bourne and wish she had stayed in Boston with nothing more on her mind than being Sarah's mother. That had been two years ago now and the car hadn't been new even then. Sarah could fold herself easily enough behind the steering wheel because she wasn't a very tall girl, but some of the men she knew had a lot of trouble winding themselves up into a small enough ball to get into the passenger seat beside her. Paul simply hated travelling any distance in her car.

The thought of Paul brought a frown to her brow. She had never deliberately deceived Paul before and she felt badly about it. It didn't matter how many times in the last couple of days she had told herself it was for his own good, she still felt guilty every time he came to mind.

They had shared an uneasy meal on Wednesday night. Usually they went to the local take-away and each paid their own share of the bill, but on Wednesday Paul had refused to eat anything like a hamburger, simply because he associated all such food with America and Americans.

"We're eating Italian tonight," he had told her. "I've made up my mind."

Sarah hadn't argued. She hadn't even mentioned the number of calories Paul had put away, eating his meal in a dour silence.

"How long's that fellow staying?" he had shot at her, bringing to an abrupt end the game she had been playing with herself that she was a Master—or was it Mistress?—of wine and was testing some new creation, sniffing at the bouquet and whirling the pretty red liquid round in her glass. Nobody would now even know her opinion of the glass of plonk that came disguised in a bottle labelled Red Italian Table Wine.

"I don't know," she had said.

"Are you going out with him again?"

"I haven't been out with him at all yet."

Paul had glared at her. "What about last night?"

Sarah's guilt feelings were forgotten. "What *about* last night?" she had repeated.

"He went home with you?"

"So?"

"What d'you know about him? You were a fool to show him where you live."

"You know where I live," she had pointed out.

"You know I won't hurt you," he had said.

"Do I?" She had needed the reassurance because, quite suddenly, she hadn't been at all sure that he wouldn't hurt her if she were to defy him and go all out to encourage James Foxe to get to know her.

"Don't be silly!" Paul had reproved her.

She had wondered then if she really knew him any better than he knew her. Had they only been making use of each other because neither of them liked to be seen round town on their own?

It was then that she had decided not to tell Paul anything about the coming weekend with her mother. She hadn't felt able to cope with his disapproval, not if she wanted to go on liking him. And she did. Paul had been a very important person in her life for months now. It wasn't in her nature to go round hurting the people of whom she was fond.

James Foxe's only visible luggage was a paperback he had thrust into his jacket pocket.

"Don't you wear pyjamas?" Sarah teased him as he made a surprisingly good job of making himself comfortable on the seat beside her.

"Always, when I'm staying in a strange house." His face creased into the smile that had intrigued her from the first moment she had seen him. "You don't have to be afraid I'll disgrace you by wandering around stark naked.

Sarah grinned. He hadn't met her mother yet. "Where are they?" she asked him.

He reached for his overcoat, producing a sponge

bag out of one pocket and a pair of pyjamas neatly packaged in plastic from another.

"Satisfied?"

"I'm sure you'll make the perfect guest," she said.

"I hope so." He wasn't smiling now and his eyes were an inky blue, far darker than she had remembered. "I appreciate your hospitality."

Well, she knew that. She knew how she would feel in a foreign country, not knowing anyone, if someone asked her to their home.

"My mother's tickled pink that you're coming," she told him. Now was the moment to warn him about her mother's obsession, but she couldn't think of the right words to make it into a joke.

"I suppose you usually take Paul with you?" James said.

Her fingers tightened on the steering wheel. "Not often."

"Don't you go about as a couple?"

She slowed at a crossroads, looking right, and left, and right again. "Whoever told you that?"

"Paul did, as a matter of fact."

Sarah's mouth was dry. "Oh?"

"I gathered you hadn't told him about this weekend," James went on dryly. "You don't have to worry, I didn't tell him either."

"I wasn't worried," she said.

"I might have told him," James went on, just as if she hadn't spoken, "only I had the feeling I was being warned off. It didn't seem to me to be any of his business, so I told him I steered my own course, no matter what the opposition. If I got the situation wrong, I'm sorry."

"Paul and I are only friends."

James smiled lazily. "Have you told him that recently?"

"All the time," said Sarah. She hadn't spelt it out, she added silently, but it shouldn't have been necessary. Paul knew that as well as she did.

James gave her a disbelieving look. "Just keep it in mind that I'm no sucker when it comes to money—or women!" he said.

Sarah stiffened. "What's that supposed to mean?" she demanded.

"Why don't you let the poor sap off the hook?"

Sarah turned off the main road, deciding suddenly to go across the fens all the way to Wisbech. There would be less traffic on the narrow, curly roads that traversed the black, rich, hard-won fields where almost anything grew, making a lot of money for the local farmers. If James was going to ask questions like that, she wouldn't have much concentration left over for her driving. It would serve her right if she landed them both in one of the many drains which took the water in no apparent order, first into the rivers and then into the sea.

"What makes you think I have him on a hook?" she challenged.

"Isn't it obvious?"

"Not to me."

She hadn't known how close she was to losing her temper, but she thought if he made one more reference to Paul she would surely crown him. She might even turn him out of the car to walk all the way back to Boston too. And there weren't many buses these days that went anywhere where they were wanted.

"He thinks it's only a matter of time before you agree to marry him," James went on, oblivious to his danger.

Sarah stopped the car. "That does it," she said. "Did he tell you that?"

He was wary now, but underneath it all she knew he was laughing at her. She supposed there was something funny about her impotent fury, but he wouldn't find it funny when she'd finished telling him a thing or two!

"He told me quite a lot about you," he said.

"I'll bet. What a cosy time you must have had together! I can tell you quite a lot about him too—"

"He didn't know about Richard."

"Richard is *business!* So are you!"

"Is that why you invited me home for the week-end?"

"That was because you're a stranger in the land!"

He chuckled. It was a warm sound of pure amusement. "So are most of your customers, I should imagine."

They were, but they didn't come alone. They brought their spouses, or their children, or a friend, and they left her to get on with the job by herself and mail the results to them when she had finished. It hadn't been like that with James Foxe. He had practically moved into her office with her.

"Do you want me to drive?" he asked her.

"Heaven forbid!" she muttered. "These roads are narrow enough without you wanting to go along on the wrong side!"

"You don't sound as though you trust me," he said teasingly.

"I must, or I wouldn't have invited you home for the weekend," she said, tartly. "But that doesn't give you authority to plan my social life. I'll make a bargain with you. I won't interfere with your friendships if you don't interfere in mine."

"Paul is no friend to you. I'm not sure I want to be either."

She was hurt. What had Paul told him to make him feel like that?

She started up the car again and drove rather too fast past one of the churches that nestled in the few trees that broke up the fields. "Paul and I have known each other for a long time," she murmured.

"He wants to be your lover."

Sarah hesitated in changing gears, and there was a grinding noise that brought her back to reality in a hurry.

"Don't be ridiculous!" she threw at him. "Paul wouldn't know how!"

James looked smug and completely at his ease. "That's the unkindest thing I've ever heard you say." He smiled at her.

Sarah blushed. She hadn't meant to say anything like that about Paul. She hadn't even wanted to think it.

"Stick around, I haven't got started on you yet!" she invited. She felt better. Much better. "And don't pay any attention to anything my mother says to you. She has a fixation about getting her only daughter married—"

"Understandable."

"I'm perfectly all right as I am!"

He shook his head. "Playing the field is all right for a time, but not when the right person for you comes along. I want to be your lover too."

"Good," she approved, not believing a word of it. "Tell that to my mother and you'll be disqualified out of your own mouth. My mother wants a white wedding and all the trimmings."

"She sounds a nice lady."

"She is. I have a nice stepfather too. David Bourne. He comes from Boston too, but he moved to Wisbech a while ago. They live in a gorgeous Georgian house overlooking the river. It was built by one of the many Quaker families who made their fortunes round here."

"What does your stepfather do?"

"He's a vet."

"A veterinarian? He treats animals?"

She nodded. "He prefers a farm practice to peoples' pets and he gets a better balance in Wisbech than he did in Boston, or so he says. I think he made the change because my mother had lived with my father in Boston and he wanted to give her something else to think about. She's always been Mrs. Bourne in Wisbech. When she comes to Boston, most of her old friends still think of her as Mrs. Gilbert."

They got onto safer topics after that. Sarah filled in a good deal of the time telling about the fens and explaining the intricacies of their drainage. She knew a lot of frightening stories about the Fen Slodgers of old, who had wrung a living out of the wetland before they had been drained and become respectable.

They were coming in to Wisbech now and Sarah gave up talking to concentrate on the traffic and a place to park that would be somewhere near where her mother lived. She was lucky, arriving before either of the boys and taking possession of the carport her stepfather had built for the convenience of their visitors.

"It isn't often I get the drop on them!" she crowed, banging on the back door to be let in. "They won't half carry on when they have to go to car park and use their legs for once."

"They?" James asked her.

"Simon and Alan. They live next door, and David said they could park over here if nobody else was expected. They don't count me as anybody—I'm just the daughter of the house."

James looked amused. "You like your stepfather, don't you?" he said.

"You will too," Sarah assured him cheerfully. "He's a darling!"

"And Simon and Alan?"

Sarah wondered what to say about them. She was saved from having to answer at all by her mother's appearance in the doorway, looking as impeccable as ever. She saw the car at once and frowned.

"Alan and Simon usually park—"

"Not tonight!"

Mrs. Bourne smiled her sweetest smile. "I wonder why you have to quarrel with all your young men. A spoonful of honey—" Her gaze fell on James and her jaw dropped. "Is *this* your American?" she demanded.

"James Foxe," Sarah mumbled. "My mother, Mrs. Bourne."

"My dear, if you can bring someone like this home with you, perhaps you will get away with parking on the boys' patch after all."

Sarah was not pleased by the compliment. "Mr. Foxe is descended from one of Mr. Cotton's daughters. We're not likely to have much in common."

Mrs. Bourne's attention was otherwise engaged. "So is my husband," she told James, "so consider yourself one of the family. Come in, my dear! I don't know why Sarah is hovering on the doorstep—and the back door at that. D'you mind coming through the kitchen? No, no, don't worry about that. Simon and Alan will bring in Sarah's luggage for her when they arrive, if they're not too cross about where she's left her car, that is. They've got used to parking there—"

"They can walk as well as I can," Sarah insisted. "And I'll bring in my own bag. The usual room, Mother?"

"Yes, darling. I've made up the one next door for Mr. Foxe—or may I call you James? My name is Betty. So much friendlier, don't you think?"

"Indeed," James responded politely. He gathered up Sarah's bag with a no-nonsense look about him and marched into the house in his hostess's wake.

Sarah followed more slowly. She couldn't remember any occasion when her mother had wanted to be on first-names terms with a friend of hers. Mrs. Bourne believed in the formalities of life as much as she believed in having meals on time and in the dining room. She had been appalled to learn that her daughter frequently ate on her knees in front of the television.

"Are you always called James?" Sarah asked him as they gained the landing of the magnificent Georgian house.

"Not always, no. Some people call me Jim."

"Or Jimbo?"

"Not often."

She believed him. She knew well what it was that her mother saw in him. She felt the same tug on her femininity herself, more so probably because she wasn't a happily married woman in her middle years. What she didn't understand was why his very obvious virile masculinity should annoy her so much. In his presence, she threw up defences against him in a way that alarmed her. She liked men, enjoyed their company more than most of her girl friends, yet she wasn't sure she liked James at all. She'd open her mouth to tease him as she would have done anyone else, but the words wouldn't come. They stuck fast in her throat, leaving her feeling gauche and a dead bore to boot.

He liked the room that had been allotted to him. It overlooked the pleasant walled garden behind the house, which at the moment was full of autumn-burnished bushes and dahlias, bowed over with the weight of their blooms, which had always been one of her mother's favourite flowers. A Virginia creeper on the wall added a romantic touch to the scene, and Sarah stood beside him at the window for a moment, enjoying it as much as he was.

"There's a very famous house just down the road—Peckover House—owned by the National Trust. We could go and see it tomorrow, if you like."

"Is it anything like this one?"

"Very like. Only there, the floors are still scrubbed

by hand. It has original doors and so do we, and so on. David has his own furniture, which isn't Georgian at all. The furniture over there is mostly Georgian and all of it suitable, but it wasn't given with the house. It was put in afterwards."

James turned and looked at her and she could feel the force of his smile pass right through her being. Instinctively, she put a hand on the windowsill to give herself support. She didn't smile back. She couldn't. She needed everything she had to go on standing there and not take to her heels and run.

"I feel very much at home here," he said. "We have Colonial houses at home very like this one. I lived in one as a boy."

"Where do you live now?" she asked him.

"I have an apartment in the centre of Boston."

A crash came from downstairs, followed by some very masculine swearing.

"My car!" Sarah gasped.

She was down the stairs as fast as she could go, just in time to see Alan and Simon making their escape into the next-door house.

"Hey, you two, what've you done to my car?"

They came back, all smiles. As twins, they looked uncannily alike, but they had never been able to deceive Sarah by pretending to be one another, as they did many people.

"Hullo, Sarah. Didn't know you were staying this weekend."

They stepped forward and kissed her on the cheek, one standing on either side of her as they tried to turn her round to face the road. James, coming more slowly after her, was just in time to see her put an arm round either strong neck and threaten to bang their heads together.

"What have you done with my car?" she repeated.

"We only moved it a little bit to make room for our new Sierra. Now, you wouldn't be selfish about the only parking space around, would you, Sarah? Not a nice, kind-hearted girl like you!"

"We'll see," said Sarah.

She pulled herself free, stalking over to where the two cars were now parked. Her own, as far as she could see, had been lifted bodily to the rear of the carport, turned to make it impossible to come or go, and the Sierra had been parked behind it.

"How am I supposed to get out?"

Simon wrapped his arms about her, nuzzling his face into her neck. "You don't have to worry, Sarah, honestly! When you want to leave, we'll put it back for you, exactly as it was, a little pimple in the middle of the largest carport in the street!"

"That's all very well, but what was that crash we heard?"

Alan came and joined the group. Their affectionate embraces caused her hair to come down her back and she began to wish they'd leave her alone.

"The truth is, darling Sarah, your car was a little heavier than we'd thought. We got it into place and then—we dropped it. But it's all right. You've always said it has very good springs . . ."

"If you've hurt my car—" she sputtered.

The two young men looked at each other and laughed.

"You'll put it right, and you'll pay for the damage out of your own pockets!"

"Have we ever let you down?" they reproached her.

"Often!"

But she was laughing too now, and when they kissed her again, as warm and as cuddly as two young puppies, she kissed them too, mussing up their neatly brushed hair as they had hers, as much at home with them as she would have been had they been her brothers.

When they'd gone, she stood looking after them, vainly trying to wind her hair back up into a neat knot at the back of her neck.

"May I help?" James asked frostily.

She had forgotten all about him for the moment. Her spirits sank until her feet felt as though they were weighted down with lead. She wished with all her heart the last few moments back again because she knew exactly what he was thinking. She supposed she could blame his Puritan ancestors for that! Then she began to get mad. What had she done, after all? Alan and Simon were only two charming boys, and if she didn't mind their horsing about, why should he?

"No, you can't!"

She tried to walk back into the house, but he stood in front of her, as immovable as a brick wall. In vain did she try to push him out of her way. In vain did she try to dodge her way round him. She took a deep breath and faced up to him, giving him sour look for sour look.

"It's a wonder they didn't do themselves a damage, lifting cars . . ." Her voice died away, her mouth suddenly dry. "What's the matter?" she asked him.

He reached round her with one hand and tipped her

up against the hardness of his chest, holding her there with an ease that brought a whispered protest to her lips.

"You're free enough with your kisses," he said. "Why don't you try kissing me?"

She knew exactly what to do. With any other man she would have done it. She would have laughed and made a joke of it, kissing him on the cheek, and laughing again as if she hadn't a care in the world. With this man she could only stare at him, her eyes dark with a kind of fear she had never felt before, trying to swallow the lump in her throat that was threatening to strangle her.

His lips moved against hers with an unexpected gentleness and she felt a rush of pleasure as his tongue met hers at the entrance to her mouth.

"It's a pity anyone will do," he said sadly as he released her. "Any man, that is. You kiss very nicely, Sarah Gilbert. Practice makes perfect, as they say."

Chapter Four

Sarah spent Saturday morning avoiding James Foxe. This was made easier by her mother's delight in their guest. What they did all morning Sarah didn't enquire. She herself had spent a miserable few hours wondering how to persuade Alan and Simon to take James off her hands for the afternoon. In this ploy she was defeated by her stepfather. He sat down at the lunch table, beaming a smile at all and sundry.

"Mission accomplished!" he said to his wife, rubbing his hands together. "Now then, you two, see you're back for tea in good time. Betty and I have a surprise for you!"

Sarah pulled herself together with an effort. "Cucumber sandwiches?" she suggested.

"Probably," her mother agreed, "but that wouldn't be any surprise. What else does one have for tea?"

"Cut and come again cake," David said, grinning.

"*Thin* bread and butter with homemade jam," Sarah added.

They both enjoyed her mother's formal and very English teas, usually served with a choice of teas in silver teapots and in the kind of cups that most people kept in a cupboard behind glass doors and never used at all.

"You're teasing me," her mother said. "Just for that, *you* can cut the bread and butter!"

"Done," said Sarah easily. That would keep her in the kitchen and safely out of the way for a good long time.

"It's new bread," her mother warned her.

"All the better," said Sarah.

She was not to escape James that afternoon, however. He had her jacket ready and was standing, waiting, in the hall when she came downstairs hoping that the coast was clear.

"Where are we going?" she protested as he put her jacket over her shoulders and hurried her out of the front door.

"You promised to show me Peckover House. Why not now?"

"That was before . . ."

He slid his fingers behind her bun, turning her face to his. His touch sent prickles down her spine and she was very much afraid that he knew it.

"Now you can forget about everyone else. I'll keep you too busy."

"What if my legendary susceptibility doesn't extend to you?" she demanded crossly.

He pulled gently on the lobe of her ear. "I think I can hold your attention for as long as necessary. Shall we go?"

James was interested in the fireplaces and their elaborate chimneypieces. "We used to have one just like that when I was a boy," he remembered.

"The Quakers believed in good, plain exteriors," Sarah commented, "but they let themselves rip inside. David's house was built for a Quaker family also. They were bankers, like the Peckovers, but they couldn't have been so successful, for they sold the house a little while later, while the Peckovers went on living here for a hundred and fifty years."

"Come here often, do you?" James asked her.

She made a face at him. "What if I do? I like to see something of my mother, but she and David appreciate some time to themselves. They're very happy together. My mother has a knack of being happy. She gives a lot—too much, I sometimes think, but we come from different generations."

"Meaning you'll give less?"

She thought about it, her head on one side. "Not less," she decided, "but differently. My mother believes in what she calls man management. It works for her. I prefer to meet on a more equal basis."

James grinned. "Was it your mother's idea to move to Wisbech?"

Sarah put a finger up to her lips, her eyes dancing. "Don't you dare tell David! He thinks he arranged the whole thing."

"And you? Would you ever leave Boston?"

"I might. Who knows? At the moment I'm very happy doing what I'm doing there. If I couldn't make a living, though, I might be tempted to take ship to Australia and see what my ancestors built there."

"You wouldn't come to the United States?"

"Not me!" she claimed, though she wasn't half as certain as she sounded.

"You don't feel you have anything in common with us?"

She shrugged her shoulders. "I've always wanted to see Australia. On July Fourth, you'd think our Boston was a bit of America, there are so many stars and stripes being waved and flown from peoples' windows. You'd think the only important thing that ever happened was that a few people fell foul of the established church and took themselves off!"

She was surprised at herself even while she was speaking. It didn't sound like her at all. She had always liked the Americans who flocked to Boston every year, looking up their ancestors. She wouldn't make much of a living without them and, if that weren't enough, she had always been grateful to them for their immediate friendliness, their willingness to enjoy anything that was on offer, and their generosity with themselves and their money that made dealing with them one of the best things about her working day.

"I see," James said. He sounded hurt. "You really have got it in for us, haven't you?"

She wanted to deny it, but it was one of the few defences she had left against him. If he knew how close she was to thinking him the best thing that had happened to her for a long, long time, he'd know how easy it would be for her to accept him as a lover. She didn't even think that her mother would think too badly of her for it . . .

"I just prefer Australians," she said aloud.

"Just one more thing." James took her arm. "How many Americans, or Australians, have you known?"

She could have given him the lie direct, making up the first number to come into her head, but the look in his eyes made her think twice about that. She felt an unaccustomed heat in her cheeks and wished she had the strength of mind to turn away and not answer him at all.

"Not many," she said at last.

"How many?" he insisted.

She licked dry lips. "None."

His triumph was very hard to bear. "I'm the first American you've ever kissed?"

"I *like* Australians!" She dodged the question.

"But you don't ask them home to meet your mother!"

"I only asked you because I felt sorry for you, on your own in a strange country. It certainly wasn't to give you ideas—"

"I'd already done my thinking about you."

"And come to the conclusion that any man would do for me!"

He was smiling now, a complacent smile that was nicely calculated to make her lose her temper.

"There's hope for you yet," he remarked, "if you're trying to tell me that I've succeeded in getting your whole attention to myself. My competition may not mind your thinking of two things at once, but when you're with me, you'll sing and dance only for me! Is that so bad?"

She looked at him from under her lashes, her eyes very green. "You ask a lot for a week or so's companionship," she mocked him. "I thought Americans were better wooers!"

His face relaxed into a smile that made her want to smile back at him. "Were you expecting boxes of chocolates and roses out of season? I told you, I'm very careful with my money."

"A tightwad!" she accused him, pleased by the Americanism that rose so easily to her lips.

"I thought you'd approve," he teased her.

"Oh, I do, I do! I can go and pick myself some roses in my mother's garden any time. Some of them go on blooming until Christmas time."

It might have been her imagination but she could have sworn that his glance softened into something like real pleasure.

"I'll pick one for you to wear in your hair and wow whoever comes to tea," he offered.

"What makes you think anyone is coming to tea?"

"Your mother hinted as much. A nice, friendly lady, your mother. I'd always heard the English were reserved and difficult to know, but it isn't true of her—"

"It was I who asked you for the weekend!" Sarah didn't know why she should be indignant over her mother's compliment. It may have been because there was an implicit comparison between her mother and herself and she, as usual, had come out the loser.

He was as good as his word about the rose. He

came in from the garden with a copper-coloured burgeoning bud between his fingers which he spent a long time fixing into place, curving it over the generous bun she wore at the back of her neck. When he'd done, he lifted her hair and touched his mouth to her nape.

"Very pretty!" he commented. His lips moved to her jawline and from there to her mouth.

She stepped away from him. "I'm more choosey than you suppose!"

"Where I'm concerned?"

"Definitely where you're concerned!"

He laughed, catching her up against him in a way she could only think of as being masterful. She tried to dislike the helpless feeling it gave her—with a singular lack of success. She wanted to laugh also, laugh for the sheer joy of living.

"It wouldn't take much to prove you wrong, but this isn't the right time or place. You won't mind if I snatch a quick kiss though, will you?"

She was in no position to deny him. Her heart hammered a warning message but she paid no attention to it. All her faculties were fully engaged in acquitting herself with a modicum of dignity. She had to make it clear to him that she could take him or leave him alone.

His mouth moved against hers, his tongue finding entry with an ease that exasperated her. She tried to turn her head away, but it was far too sweet to lean against the hardness of his chest, to run her fingers through his hair, and to take her pleasure from him while she could.

It wasn't for long. His ears, quicker than hers,

heard the tea trolley in the hall outside and he pushed
her away from him, hurrying to open the door for her
mother. Sarah could only admire his coolness, even
while she resented it. The very last thing she felt like
was entertaining a whole lot of strangers for tea.

"Did I interrupt something?" her mother asked
cheerfully. She gave her daughter a thoughtful look.
"Darling, a little fresh lipstick may improve things.
James can help me make the tea." She watched as
Sarah prepared to leave the room, deliberately avoiding any contact with James Foxe. "I like the rose," she
continued, her voice vague and slightly amused. "Isn't
it the Spanish who have a whole language of flowers in
their hair? Or is it the Polynesians?"

James was as amused as her mother. "That one
means hands off!" he decreed. "D'you think Alan and
Simon will get the message?"

"Paul is the one you need to worry about," Sarah's
mother commented.

James took over the tea tray with a jaunty step,
pushing it close to the sofa where Mrs. Bourne usually
sat.

"The trick with your daughter is to stay around.
Paul isn't here and I am!"

Sarah didn't mind being teased. She was used to it.
So the burning anger, accompanied by a sense of
injustice that was bigger than she was, was as shocking
to her as her indignation that James hadn't minded
her mother's knowing they had been kissing. Sarah
supposed she shouldn't mind either. She couldn't
understand why she did, unless it was because it
undermined her whole stance that James was not a

friend, certainly not a potential lover, but merely an acquaintance whom she had taken pity on for no better reason than that the laws of hospitality demanded it.

Her mother was already inclined to think there was more to it than that. She wanted to think so because she didn't like Paul and she thought James something extraordinary. Sarah had tried telling both her and David that it was because James was the sort of person television had taught them to admire, the hero of a thousand powerful episodes of imports, whereas Paul was someone real, someone who lived and breathed on the streets of England. They had laughed the idea to scorn.

"My dear girl," her mother had said, "what a charming, romantic idea. You just keep remembering that it's the television hero who always gets the girl."

"He wouldn't in real life!" Sarah had maintained.

"I shouldn't be too sure of that," Mrs. Bourne had said, her eyes on David at the time. Sarah had seen the flash of intimacy that had passed between them and she'd been tempted to admit her mother might be right. She didn't want to spend the rest of her life with Paul. There would be no intimate glances of understanding with him. Paul never did understand what all the fuss was about when she blew her top, and anything more fervent than the casual affection that lay between them would have embarrassed him terribly.

Whereas, with James . . .

Glancing out the window, Sarah was startled to see a huge car crossing the bridge and parking outside the house. An American car! On these roads it looked twice as big as life-size, and difficult to manage. In contrast to her own flea, it looked almost funny.

The front door opened and her mother and James went out into the street to greet the people getting out of the car. The driver was an elegantly dressed girl cast very much in the same mould as James. At a pinch, she could have been English, though she would have stood out in a crowd in any country. Rather as her brother did.

"Hi, you devil!" she called out to him. "Where is she?"

"Mary Beth! I thought you were coming on your own!"

"And leave Pete behind?"

"I don't count Pete—"

"That's the story of his life! Poor old Pete! Louise, here, couldn't wait to see inside a real English home. You don't mind, do you? The only people we have to visit at Mildenhall is each other."

Riveted by the scene below her, Sarah could see that James did mind. Louise was as affectionate as she was beautiful, in a southern belle fashion. It was hard to believe that she and Mary Beth came from the same country, they were so different in style, in speech—even, Sarah suspected, in their outlook on life.

She leaned a little further out of the window to see Louise wind herself round James's arm. They obviously knew each other very well indeed! It was left to Mary Beth to shake hands with her hostess and to introduce the uniformed Pete as her husband. So James wasn't on his own in a strange land at all! He had a brother-in-law stationed over here, a sister to make him feel at home, and a past, maybe even a *present,* girl friend to take care of everything else! And he hadn't breathed a word to her that he had anyone at all over here!

Sarah swept down the stairs, her head held high. She stopped only long enough to be introduced to Mary Beth and Pete, and to exchange a distant nod with Louise, who wasn't going to be diverted from her single-minded pursuit of James even for the sake of being polite.

"Where are you going?" Betty Bourne called after her daughter as she swept regally out the front door.

"Did you want me to make the tea before I go?" Sarah asked, not even breaking her step.

"No—only where are you going? I told you we had people coming to tea!"

Sarah walked on as if she hadn't heard her. She caught sight of Alan and Simon coming out of their house.

"Hey, you two, I want my car!"

"Now?"

"Now," she confirmed.

"But, Sarah darling, we have a date. Come with us, do, but don't ask us to get your car out right now."

"Where are you going?"

They grinned. "We're off to the flicks. There's a good film on for once. Coming?"

Sarah tried to make up her mind, but she didn't know what she wanted to do. All she knew was that nothing was going to induce her to go back and make polite conversation to James's family and friend. If he'd told her they were coming—

"Sarah!"

"Someone wants to catch your attention," Alan said unnecessarily. "Slow up, Sarah! Simon and I aren't in that much of a hurry! Besides, I shouldn't mind meeting your beautiful pursuer. What say you, Simon?"

"She's married!" Sarah ground out.

"Just our luck!" They sighed in unison.

Sarah turned and faced her breathless pursuer. Mary Beth silently held out the copper rosebud that had fallen from her hair.

"I thought I'd come with you," she announced frankly. "I can't stand watching Louise oozing all over Jim, especially when he does nothing to stop her. Brothers! Where are we going?"

"To the cinema." Simon grinned at her, eagerly waiting to be introduced.

"Hi, there. I'm Mary Beth Karenski. Are you friends of Sarah's?"

"We are now," Alan told her.

Mary Beth only laughed. Sarah judged she was used to having young men flatter her. She had much the same impact as her brother on the opposite sex. "Much as I'd love to go with you, I haven't the time," she told them. "Sarah and I'll just catch tea at one of those little tea shops you have over here. I'll have to be getting back after that. It took us longer to get here from Mildenhall than we expected."

Sarah suppressed a smile. It was a long time since she had taken to anyone on sight as she had to Mary Beth.

"Did James send you after me?" she asked her.

"James doesn't send me anywhere! To tell the

truth, I can't like cucumber in any form and he told me that was what we were being given for tea. I can well understand your taking off on your own."

"It wasn't quite like that," Sarah heard herself confessing. "I didn't know James had any of his family in England. I thought he was on his own—"

"And you didn't want to meet us?"

"I wanted to get used to the idea first."

Mary Beth was silent for a long moment. She watched Alan and Simon until they were out of sight, a slight frown between her eyes. "Louise doesn't mean anything—"

"Who cares about Louise?" Sarah shrugged.

"Well, I think I might if I had asked Jim for the weekend with my parents. James should have told us—"

"There's nothing to tell. I only asked James home because I thought he was on his own and didn't know anyone."

"Really?"

Sarah ignored the flustered feeling that was slowly getting the better of her. "That, and because he made your mother sound nice. I'm working on your family tree. It's very interesting."

"And that's all?"

"Yes, that's all."

Sarah felt a traitor even as she said it, yet what was there more than that? A physical attraction that she might feel with anyone who was a little out of the ordinary. And if she gave way to it, where would it get her? He was only here for a week or two and then he would be back to America, leaving her to pick up the pieces.

"Then, if it isn't Louise, what got you?" Mary Beth asked frankly.

"Nothing got me. I just felt like going out by myself—"

"With those two boys?"

It was easy to see that James had told Mary Beth a lot more than Sarah felt she needed to know about her. And when had he found the time? Sarah sniffed. She wasn't sure that she liked the idea of Mary Beth thinking her to be susceptible to any man around, as James did. She rather liked Mary Beth, and she'd have liked to have been friends with her. It was one more thing that James had ruined for her.

"They're friends of mine."

Mary Beth tucked her arm in Sarah's, just as if they'd known each other for years. "Why don't we go back and see what else your mother's offering for tea?" she suggested. "We can sit and glare at Louise together. She has the hide of a rhinoceros and won't even notice—but Jim will! I'd love to see that creature get her comeuppance! Jim is very protective of his women, you know. He won't like it if she puts your nose out of joint."

Sarah knew she was being managed in the nicest possible way, but she didn't resent it. She laughed inwardly as she thought that even her mother could take lessons from Mary Beth.

"One tea party isn't much out of all the time they can spend together when they go back to America," she said aloud.

Mary Beth looked completely blank. "But didn't Jim tell you? He's going to be here for the next year at least. He has some international case on and he's making his headquarters with us rather than over in Europe where he doesn't know anyone. Not even Louise can stick around that long, not unless he offers her a great deal more encouragement than he has in the past. It'll be up to us to see that he doesn't!"

Chapter Five

Sarah joined the queue that spilled out of the doors of the shop under the shadow of the Stump. It was a raw day, heralding winter, and she had thought to have a baked potato for her lunch while she brooded on the problem of going back another generation in James Foxe's family tree. She hadn't seen him for more than a week and she was surprised and annoyed to find she had missed him. She had been surprised when he had travelled back with her to Boston from Wisbech, supposing he would instead go on to his sister's. She had yet to discover where he was living in Boston. Of one thing she was quite certain—he wasn't staying with anyone she knew.

"Hey, Sarah, what do you want, and I'll get it for you?"

Sarah pretended not to have heard. Her relationship with Paul was not going well—to put it mildly.

All she seemed to do was quarrel these days and she couldn't understand it; quarrelling was so unlike her.

"Sarah, come out of the clouds and tell me what you're going to eat!"

Sarah frowned, feeling foolish. She'd known Paul for years and it was nothing short of ridiculous to start ignoring him now.

"I thought I'd have a baked potato, with cream cheese, and a lot of salt and pepper."

Paul shook his head at her, grinning. "All those calories!"

She didn't have to worry about calories at the moment; she was burning them off with frustration. She couldn't concentrate on her work either; nothing seemed to matter very much. Still, she could hardly tell Paul that. It wouldn't be tactful and he probably wouldn't believe her anyway.

"I don't care!" she said aloud.

Paul came out of the bursting shop with her potato in one hand and some concoction of his own in the other.

"How much do I owe you?" Sarah asked him.

"Since when have I ever asked you to pay for your own lunch?" he demanded.

"We always go Dutch," she said firmly. "If you haven't noticed, that's because I'm a very tactful girl."

"I never ask you to pay," Paul maintained moodily.

"I know you don't. As I earn every bit as much as you do, however, I'm not going to allow you to pay for my potato. You can pay when it's a special occasion."

"Like when? I haven't seen you all week."

"I've been busy."

"I'd noticed. Where have you been?"

"I went to my mother's for the weekend and I've had a lot of work on ever since."

"For that American fellow?"

"Amongst others," she admitted.

James Foxe's family tree was giving her problems. She had traced the main branch back a couple of hundred of years before they had left for America, but then they had seemingly disappeared into the sands of time. She was beginning to doubt they had originally been a Lincolnshire family at all.

"You haven't been going out with him, have you?"

"No. I haven't seen him for days. Not that it's got anything to do with you!" she added.

"Well, I wondered. You didn't turn up for the folksinging session this week and I don't enjoy it much when you're not there."

"Poor Paul," Sarah sympathised.

"At least it didn't turn into a barn dance this time. There was nobody there who can sing as you do, though. One fellow tried out a number or two, but nobody knew the words—or the tune either. Everybody was asking where you were!"

Sarah could imagine it. She felt sorry for Paul, for she knew that everyone would have been asking him where she was. And when he couldn't supply any answer they might not have said anything but their minds would have been jumping to conclusions.

"I'll be there next week," she said.

"I said you had a cold," Paul volunteered. She could tell he hadn't meant to tell her that. He must have really had his back against the wall to start telling lies, she thought. What was she supposed to say next week when they all asked her if she were feeling better?

"Couldn't you have told them the truth, that I was busy?" she demanded.

"I knew they'd all think you were with that American fellow."

"Well, I wasn't!"

She wished she had been. She wished Paul hadn't told her anything about it. It wasn't that she wanted to make comparisons between the two men. Far from it, that was the last thing she wanted to do, especially as Paul seemed to come out of it so badly. James wouldn't have resorted to lies, she was sure of it. It made her feel all the more impatient with the luckless Paul. Why couldn't he stand on his own two feet?

"I must get back to work," she said, demolishing the last of her potato. She brushed her fingers together, shivering as a cold blast of air came out of one of the passageways bearing its message that winter was coming.

"Wait a minute," said Paul. "What are you doing tonight?"

"I don't know. I thought I'd wash my hair."

"There's nothing you want to do?"

She shook her head. "Not tonight." He looked forlorn and that made her feel a beast. If he wanted her company, couldn't he ask her to do something specific for once?

"Oh well, maybe I'll see you tomorrow?"

"Maybe," she said.

She tried to throw off the memory of his hurt, doleful eyes as she hurried away from him. What Paul needed, she thought, was a nice, quiet girl who would think him absolutely marvelous and who wasn't always telling him what to do. She had a horrible suspicion that during the time they'd been going out together she had scotched what little spirit he had by going her own way, not caring particularly whether he tagged along or not. Perhaps she should have listened to him more. She was struck that she was thinking in the past tense and realised that sooner or later she was going to have to tell him that they hadn't got a future together. Nor could she think of any way of letting him down lightly. He'd look hurt and go on being there for ever unless she did something drastic. Oh why did the onset of winter always have to be so depressing?

Her office was in a state of chaos. She took one look, wrapped her coat more firmly about her, and prepared to walk down the stairs again. She would go somewhere, do something, maybe even take some photos of the land in its autumnal garb. There weren't many trees around on the fens, but the skies were often spectacular and at this time of year there were flocks of birds gathering for their flight to warmer climes, their choreography superb against the green-tinged horizons that were yet another sign that the last of summer had gone for another year.

"Missed me?"

The words cut through her thoughts and brought her up short, depriving her of breath and bringing a tingling sensation to her flesh.

"Should I have?"

She wondered why James Foxe should be able to dominate her whole office when he was not a particularly big man.

He smiled slowly. "I have three whole days," he said. "What are we going to do with them?"

She put her head on one side, holding on to her bag until her fingers showed white against the polished leather. "Well, as you can see, I'm snowed under with work—"

"Funny, I thought you were going out."

"My work frequently takes me out."

He sat on the edge of her desk, still smiling. "Getting acquainted with my ancestors? I hope they're treating you nicely?"

"Some of them." She reached round him, looking for the rough copy she had made of his mother's family tree. "I'm beginning to wonder if the family originated here at all."

He glanced down at her efforts. "Have you been to Heckington Church and had a look round there?"

"Not yet. I doubt the family were important enough to have left any monuments and the more recent records have all gone to Lincoln. I've got all the relevant ones, almost back to when the first records began."

He put out a hand, touching the bun on the nape of her neck. "You never know," he said, "we may find heaven's gate at Heckington."

"We'll find a windmill," she answered prosaically. "The last of the eight-sailed windmills in the country."

If he undid her hair and wound it round his fingers

as he had once before, she doubted they would go anywhere. It was too bad that he should come and go whenever he thought he would, without a word of explanation, and she was as glad to see him as ever.

"I don't want to go to Heckington!" she said. "I'm not ready to go to Heckington! I don't believe your family ever came from Heckington!"

"I have an automobile waiting outside," he told her. "Are you ready?"

"What automobile? What's wrong with my car?"

"It's a bit on the small side for the two of us."

"Huh!" said Sarah. "I hope yours is more practical than your sister's!"

He grinned. "That's just what Mary Beth said. She would've talked Pete out of bringing theirs over if she could. She'd been to England before; he hadn't. Mustn't frighten the horses, she said."

Sarah was incensed. "We've had cars just as long as you have!" she pointed out coldly. "Probably longer!"

He chuckled. "You're as prickly as a hedgehog! Mildenhall is fairly near Newmarket, where all your best racing stables are. Mary Beth goes all the time to see the great champions being exercised."

Sarah felt a fool. If anyone ought to know about the racing stables, it was she. Her stepfather often visited them in his capacity as veterinarian, filling in for the ones they employed on a full-time basis if any of them were away.

"Do you ride too?" she asked.

"A bit. Do you?"

She shook her head. "I haven't that kind of money.

My mother hunts sometimes now she's married to David, but her heart isn't in it. She likes the exercise, but gets quite hysterical if they actually put up a fox and run it to ground."

"Just as her daughter would?" James teased her.

"I have too much sympathy for anyone on the run to want to add to their distress," she muttered.

His eyes met hers. "You don't have to run away from me," he said.

She lifted her chin. "Why should I want to?"

"I reckon you're afraid of losing out to good old American know-how," he taunted her. "Those other men of yours don't believe in calling the shots where you're concerned, do they?"

She had no answer to that. "Perhaps I've inherited more from my mother than I thought," she retorted.

He nodded. "More than she imagines, but you won't manage me, Miss Gilbert, with soft talk and amiable ways. Action, not words, are the way to my heart."

"Then you'd better look elsewhere," she said.

"I've found what I want." Her hair came loose, falling over her shoulders in a cloud of gold silk. "Are you going to give in with a good grace?"

"Go away!" she shouted at him.

He shook his head. "The English never know when they're beaten—"

"That's why we're usually on the winning side in the end!" she said smugly.

"Not with us Americans," he retorted calmly. "Remember the Boston Tea Party? Remember—"

"All I remember is burning down the White

House," she said with dignity. "Not a bad effort seeing the greater part of our troops were otherwise engaged in Europe."

"Keep on remembering," he bade her. "You can win all the other wars, but you can't win with me!"

"What other wars?"

"Paul, Alan, and Simon, to name just three."

"I'm not at war with any one of them."

"You don't think they fancy taking over your territory?"

"That's my business—not yours!"

"No?" His eyes were alight with laughter. "You haven't been listening. I'm staking my interest here and now!"

His fingers caught in her hair and she found herself captured within the circle of his arms, a prisoner as much of her own need as of his determination. If she objected, she thought, it would be a ritual objection, without meaning, and he would know it. Far better to play along with him for a while. Nothing much could happen to her in her own office. Nothing ever had.

"It may cost you dearly," she warned him, smiling a little.

"Nothing I'm not willing to pay."

She wondered what he meant by that and suspected he thought he had matters nicely in hand. He would give her as much of himself as he wanted to and no more.

"Really?" Her smile widened. "How generous you are!"

His arms tightened about her. "Come to Holland with me next weekend? I have to go back on Sunday anyway. We could go on Friday and spend a couple of days together."

Her eyebrows rose. "Certainly not," she said.

"Why not?"

"I have my own life here. In my own small way I'm quite successful. I don't need to be talked about by all my friends and acquaintances. It wouldn't be good for business, and it'd be even worse for my social life. Boston is a very respectable town and its daughters don't go away for the weekend with strange men."

"I don't count myself a stranger," he complained, "not to you. Never to you, Sarah Gilbert. If you wanted to keep me at arm's length you shouldn't have handed me the end of the golden string."

Once again his fingers were in her hair, bunching it up in his fist until she couldn't move her head at all. She knew he was going to kiss her and her lips were burning in anticipation. She felt like the princess in the story who let down her golden hair for the prince to climb up the tower to be with her. "Did you hear what I said?" she added sharply. Anything was better than this long, terrifying silence between them.

"Words, my love. Didn't anyone ever tell you that actions speak louder than words?"

Now he was going to kiss her!

His eyes gleamed with a wicked challenge. "Why don't you kiss me?" he suggested.

The colour flooded into her face. She hadn't realised he knew how she was feeling, that he was there ahead of her when it came to her reactions to his touch and the sight and smell of him. She wondered briefly about the many women who had taught him all he needed to know about her sex and was seared by a momentary jealousy that they already knew him in a way she probably never would. Come to Holland with me, he had said, just as if it were the easiest thing in the world for her to down tools and follow him around until it was convenient for him to go back to America again without her.

"You don't deserve my kisses," she said with more spirit than she thought she had left.

His hands flattened against her back, coaxing her into being more amenable. "What a good thing we don't always get what we deserve!" he murmured.

It was bliss when his mouth touched hers. She clung to him in relief, arching herself more closely against his body. It was a passionate, compulsive coming together that took her breath away. She was drowning in delight and a warm lethargy that made it impossible to move away from him.

"You see how nice it is?" he murmured in her ear.

"Mmm." It was nice. It was more than nice; it was the best thing that had ever happened to her. "You taste nice," she said.

So many nices, she mocked herself, remembering how she had been told at school never to use the word. What did it mean? her teacher had asked. The word was meaningless. Well, it wasn't meaningless to Sarah any longer. It meant something she could never describe, no matter how many words she had to do it in. It meant the kind of happiness that she shared only with James: she had never known it with anyone else. And it was nice; it was lovely!

He held her closer still, one hand cupping her

breast and sending little rivulets of excitement through her bloodstream.

"Not in the office," she said. "Someone might come in."

She had meant to sound professional and efficient, but it didn't come out like that. Even to her own ears her voice sounded husky and more than a bit sexy, as though she didn't mean what she was saying.

"Richard?"

She laughed. "I haven't seen Richard since the day he was in to collect the proof that he was next in line for the farm. He won't be back."

"He was very affectionate, for someone who didn't mean to come back," James muttered.

"He was grateful—"

"He and who else?"

Sarah sighed. "My clients are usually nice to me. They're nice people. Mostly they bring me boxes of chocolates, or flowers, or something like that. Richard doesn't have much imagination when it comes to saying thank you."

"Don't any of them pay you for your efforts?" he demanded.

"Sure. They're often in a hurry for quick results, though, if they're only here for a few days. Hardly anyone stays around for a whole year!" she added, not without resentment, for she thought he could have told her he was staying on instead of leaving it to his sister to do so.

"I'm attached to the International Court at The Hague—"

"Then what are you doing here?"

He grinned. "You asked me home for a weekend; I thought I'd return the compliment."

"You mean Mary Beth will be in Holland?"

His smile died. "No. I'm sure she'll ask you to the base at Mildenhall if you want her to, however."

Somehow his fingers had taken hold of her wrist like a bracelet, or handcuffs, and the pressure woke her from the cocoon of warm pleasure that had surrounded her since he had taken her into his arms. He was hurting her, but he seemed quite unaware of it. He wasn't even looking at her, but over her shoulder at a paper she had left on her desk. She tried to remember what it was, but could only visualise the general chaos in which she had left everything when she had gone for lunch.

"They don't seem to get off the base much," she observed, wincing.

"Most of them don't," he agreed.

"Aren't we nice to them?" she asked. She pulled at her hand. "Let me go, James. You're hurting me."

He did so at once, rubbing the bruise he had given her with healing fingers. "I'm sorry," he apologised. "I guess that's a pointer to how much I want you to come with me. Sure you won't change your mind?"

"Quite sure."

"Yet you'll go to Mildenhall—"

"Your sister is at Mildenhall."

The lines of his face looked hard and unyielding. He didn't look angry exactly, but she could tell he was far from being pleased.

"You don't require a chaperon when you go out with Paul!" he snapped.

"I don't stay overnight with him," she pointed out gently.

"Oh, come on, sweetie, don't pretend that none of the men who hang around you all the time don't get further than a few kisses!"

She stood away from him, taking a deep breath to steady herself. If they weren't actually touching she might have found the strength to tell him what she thought of him and his filthy mind. What had she ever done to make him think she was a pushover where men were concerned?

She flicked her hair into a single rope and wound it up into its usual knot in the single, easy movement that Indian women have, a graceful, ultrafeminine motion that was as old as women have been wearing their hair long. Sarah could sit on hers if she had a mind to, for it had never been cut, not since she'd been a baby and her mother had trimmed it to give it a style.

She held out her hand for her pins, her gesture imperative and unyielding. If he could think that of her, then she could be every bit as distant as he! He put them in her palm, one at a time, looking at her out of the corners of his eyes. She thought he might apologise, but he didn't.

"Well?" he ground out.

She forced a smile. "What's sauce for the gander is sauce for the goose! Haven't you ever kissed anyone before?"

His expression was grim. She began to wish she hadn't needled him because she didn't like to think what might happen if he were to get really angry. She wasn't sure her strength of mind was all that it ought to be. She had never really wanted to go to bed with a man before, but with James . . .

"No, don't answer that!" she said. "I don't want to know!"

He looked her over from head to toe and she had no idea what he was thinking. "All right, Miss Gilbert," he said at last. "We'll play it your way. What do I have to do to become your lover?"

She gasped at the frankness of the question. Her senses reeled and she licked dry lips. *What did he have to do?* What was she going to have to do to prevent him from getting his own way?

"You—I—I don't know!"

"You won't let me court you in the usual way," he went on, in such reasonable tones she was almost conned into thinking he had forgotten all about his momentary anger. "Other people can give you chocolates and flowers, but from me you'd say I was throwing my dollars around. I try to tell you how much I want you when I kiss you, but you won't believe me. And you won't come to Holland with me in case people begin to talk. What *will* you do?"

She began to climb back into her jacket, buttoning it up as far as it would go. She wrote a note in capital letters on the pad on her desk and put it in a handy place where it could be seen in case anyone came looking for her.

"I'll go to Heckington with you," she said.

The road turned off left for the windmill. Sarah tossed up in her mind whether she should remind him that it was here that the only eight-sailed windmill had been put in order. He might not be interested in windmills and he certainly wasn't going to find any evidence of his ancestors in its shadow. She was still arguing the point with herself, when he turned off, the Mercedes he had hired cornering as smoothly and easily as any car she had ever been in.

"It looks a bit like Holland around here," he said, breaking the silence.

"A lot of Dutch people came in the past and helped drain the fens. It was their ideas that took your family to America. The Pilgrim Fathers tried to leave for Holland first, but we put them in prison instead. They only set sail across the Atlantic after that."

"Even the houses look Dutch," he remarked.

She nodded. "Dutch gables. There was a lot of to-ing and fro-ing in those days. Boston was one of the most important ports in the country. And then, of course, the reign of William and Mary put the seal on it. William was very Dutch!"

"I could do with a few more hills and trees," he said.

"But then you wouldn't have that glorious expanse of sky!" she protested. "You should see it earlier in the year, when the corn has been freshly cut and the whole land is golden. By corn I mean wheat," she added quickly, "not what you call corn."

They had come to the windmill by then. It towered over them, looking shabby and as if it had been shut up for years. Sarah undid her seat-belt and got out of the car, disappointed that they weren't to see the windmill in action, grinding the stone-ground, whole-meal flour she always used when she could get it. She marched up the steps and tried the handle of the door.

It opened to her touch and a family of angry-looking Persian kittens came pouring out of the crack.

"They look like you when you're at a loss," James told her, smiling at her efforts to return them to their home inside the windmill.

"They have yellow eyes," she said.

"And yours are green," he acknowledged. "They're as green as grass when you've just been kissed."

He bent down and shooed the kittens back inside, closing the door firmly behind them.

"And when I'm angry?" she asked him.

"I haven't made up my mind. There's plenty of time for me to find out."

She swallowed. Plenty of time? She was getting deeper in over her head every moment she was with him. She straightened her back, brushing down her skirt as she did so.

"I think we'd better get back to work," she said.

Chapter Six

Sarah had always thought the magnificent churches of Lincolnshire were spoilt by the drab colour of the stone in which they were built. Heckington was no exception. Its grandeur—and it was very grand, having been built by King Edward II's Chancellor—didn't entice her affections. Consequently, she lingered in the lee of a tree in the churchyard, persuading herself that it was getting cold and that she'd be glad when she was comfortably at home, sitting eating a lonely supper in front of the noisy gas stove that was her only means of heating her flat.

After a while, James appeared in the porch, his hands on his hips, just looking at her.

"You're supposed to be doing the work here," he said. "I only came along for the ride."

She shivered as a gust of wind pulled at her coat. "The records won't be here. I keep telling you they've been taken to Lincoln. They're all on micro-fiche these days and they only go back so far. We're looking for something impossible."

"You're wrong," said James.

He beckoned for her to come inside the church, and she did so, reluctantly, wondering at the lethargy that had seized her. She felt as though a crushing disappointment was waiting and that the only way of escaping it was to stand quite still and hope it blew over her head.

She followed him to where the medieval Easter sepulchre was situated, taking care to keep her eyes on it and not look at his broad shoulders that his jacket fitted so snugly. It was better to keep her distance, she was sure of it, and she wondered why she had ever agreed to come with him.

The sepulchre was carved with sleeping soldiers, three women, an angel and the risen Christ. The interior seemed to have been re-roofed and was green and dim as the result of having been indifferently glassed.

"Before I go back to the States I'm going to make a grand tour of the village churches of England," James said with enthusiasm. "Every one of them seems to have some treasure to make the visit worthwhile."

Sarah nodded vaguely, not really taking in what he was saying. Now that she'd refused to go to Holland, there was nothing else she wanted to do. Even when she didn't look at him, James Foxe filled her vision, and she felt a great loneliness when she thought of life without him.

"However," James went on, "it wasn't that I called you in to see. Have a look at this!"

There was a simple plaque on the wall, deteriorating with age, and only just legible if one knew what one was looking for. It was written in Latin, and might once have had a bronze representation in the middle. Sarah stared at it, translating the broken letters in her mind.

"You're right," she admitted at last. "Your family came from Heckington. I'd made up my mind you were tenant farmers from over Grantham way, if you didn't come originally from the Netherlands."

James grinned. "Jumping ahead of your evidence?"

"Playing my hunches," she corrected. "Mostly, it works pretty well."

"And instead we were gentlemen of this parish?"

"Looks like it." She gestured towards the founder's tomb, carved with a mass of foliage, angels and saints. "Maybe they were part of Richard de Potesgrave's entourage and settled here."

James fingered the plaque with loving fingers. "This'll give them a kick back home. How do we find out?"

Sarah made another attempt to pull herself out of her lethargy. "I'll find out," she promised him. "There are records of Edward II's court and I may find a mention there. Those archives don't make easy reading—"

"Worrying about your fee?"

She shook her head. "It takes time, though, when you go this far back. Don't expect miracles."

His eyes narrowed as he looked at her. "I never know what to expect from you."

She was a stranger to herself right now. "I'll come over by myself and see the vicar. Sometimes there are records going way back, telling one all about the monuments in a church."

"Why not now?" James urged her.

"I'll need to make an appointment. Don't rush me, James. Americans are always in such a hurry."

He looked as bleak as the colour of the stone. "You still see me as an American rather than just as a person, don't you?" he accused her.

"Well, you're not English!" she flared.

He went on looking at her. "It'll be strange if we find our families had the same beginnings. What will you hide behind then, Sarah?"

She ignored the question. It wasn't worth answering, she told herself. She had no need to hide. The only thing that bothered her was this unaccountable depression that gripped her. She knew perfectly well how it could be relieved, but she wouldn't admit as much. If she did, it could only be the first in a whole series of admissions, and where would she be then?

"I think I'll go back to the car," she said.

"Aren't you well?"

It was tempting to say she was not, but Sarah was not a liar by nature, not even when it came to the small, everyday social lies. Still, she always managed to look guilty. She could never remember from one day to the next what it was that she'd said, and lying was only a way out of an awkward situation.

"I'm perfectly well." She didn't add thank you. She didn't have anything to thank him for. She glowered at him instead, catching the sudden amusement with which he was regarding her.

"You know what's the matter with you?" he said with enviable confidence, "You're cross because I brought you to Heckington exactly as promised, when you'd much rather be doing something else."

She swallowed. "Like what?" she challenged.

He picked up her hand by one finger, caressing the sides of it with his own. It was a sensuous movement, and she bit her lip, hoping he didn't know how quickly the fire from his touch was spreading through her veins. Icy cold only a short time earlier, she was now overheated and in need of a breath of fresh air.

"Do I have to tell you that?"

She thought she'd rather he didn't. Was it so obvious—was *she* so obvious?—that he could tell the effect he was having on her? She felt bathed in a heat that wasn't entirely embarrassment. It was a shock that physical desire could be so strong as to completely undermine her usually sunny nature and turn her into a moody, volatile creature she couldn't recognise and wasn't at all sure she knew how to deal with.

She chattered away the whole way out of the church. She had no idea what she said. She thought it must have been something about the weather and something about the fineness of medieval carving as represented by the Easter sepulchre. "Maybe an ancestor of yours was the artisan who created it?" she ended.

"I think I'd call him an artist," he said.

"I don't think there was any difference in those days. Where are we going now?"

"Home," he said.

Boston wasn't his home, of course, at least not this Boston. She wondered why he had said it. It was home for her, more or less. Now that her mother lived at Wisbech, she thought of that as home too. People

meant more to her than places; they always would.
James Foxe could mean more than any other if she
wasn't careful. He was the one person who might
persuade her to exchange one Boston for another.
Only, he didn't want that. He was marking time while
he spent his year over here, and she would do well to
remember that. Who knew whom he had waiting for
him back home? There was bound to be someone.
Sarah couldn't imagine anyone as alive, as virile as
James having nobody caring about him, waiting for
him to come back to her.

She forced a smile. "Home?" she repeated, willful-
ly misunderstanding him. "All the way to your sister?"

"All the way to your home," he said.

He held the door of the car open for her, tucking
her skirt in beside her before closing it. She sat
crouched against the door, trying to ignore how badly
she wanted to put out a hand and run it down his arm,
just for the fun of touching him. She wanted to do that
more than anything else right now.

He was as tense as she was as he got in beside her.
She watched him turn on the ignition and release the
brake, sucking her lower lip in between her teeth to
keep herself calm.

"What will we do when we get there?" she asked,
breaking the silence with a question she knew would
have been far better to keep to herself.

"If I can keep my hands off you for long enough,
you can make me a cup of tea and we'll toast some
crumpets in front of the fire. Later on, I'll take you
out to dinner. How's that?"

"Lovely," she said.

It wasn't only he who had to keep his hands to himself, she thought with a wry smile. If she asked him in would she ever get him out again? Worse, would she want to?

"There's a baker over there," he said. "I'll pick up some crumpets."

He came back in triumph, with the crumpets in a paper bag dangling from his fingers. He threw them onto her lap and got back into the car, moving off quickly with the firm, decisive movements she had come to think of as being part of him. If he decided to kiss her, there was very little she would be able to do about it. And even less she would want to do, a mocking voice said in her head.

He had mastered the geography of Boston quicker than most of their visitors. He knew exactly where he was going, parking the car in a side street she thought only she knew about. Her own car was a couple of spaces along, not far from the still narrower street where she lived. Perhaps, she thought, she ought to take him back to her office. There was no reason why they shouldn't toast the crumpets there, and she could make tea. She was still dithering when he took the crumpets from her and held out his hand for her key.

"No wonder you were complaining of the cold back there," he said. "The wind's changed. It smells of winter."

She put her hand in her pocket and drew out her latch-key. She had a rather pretty fob attached that symbolised the world at one with itself. He glanced at it, curious, and then at her.

"So we're all related, are we? I hope you'll remember that."

"Someone gave it to me," she replied defensively. "It fits in with my work."

"Another satisfied client?"

She gritted her teeth. "Yes."

"I'll bet! What was his name?"

"She was another American, like yourself. I think she came from Rhode Island. She was living there all the time we were in touch. I never actually met her. I do a lot of my work by letter. I advertise in both the American and the Australian presses."

She hoped he felt a fool, but she wouldn't rely on it. He had a determined look, as if he meant to get his own way, and that made her nervous. It would be better when she'd made up her own mind exactly how far she was prepared to go with him, she consoled herself. At the moment she didn't feel in control of the situation in any way. Far from it. She could feel her resolution slipping away from her, leaving her in a state of flux, able to respond but not to initiate anything, not even the making of tea.

James had no such difficulty. He had lit the gas fire and had put the kettle on before she had even taken off her coat.

"Butter," he said. "Crumpets do need real butter. I hope you're not one of these health cranks that never has any in the house?"

She joined him in the kitchen, getting an unopened packet of butter out of the tiny fridge she kept on a handy shelf so that it didn't use up any of the strictly limited counter space.

"New Zealand butter. I wouldn't have anything else," she murmured, slapping it down beside him.

"Good enough. We're in business. You can set to

work toasting the crumpets, while I find what's needed out here. You don't seem to keep much food in stock."

"There isn't room. I can always pick up what I want on the way home."

"Or eat out with one of your swains?"

"That too," she said. What business of his was it anyway? She was free to go out with whomever she liked. She *liked* Paul. "Paul and I—"

"And who else?" James demanded.

Sarah shut her mouth, pulling her lips into a tight line. What was the matter with him? Did he expect her to have seen no one and to have been nowhere until he had come upon her in her office that day?

"Half the town, I daresay," he rumbled on. "The male half!"

"Of course!" she muttered crossly.

"With Alan and Simon for weekends?"

"I like to keep busy."

He brought the tea-tray through from the tiny kitchenette. He looked more determined than ever. Sarah wished she could control the flare of excitement that passed through her at the mere sight of him. How easy life would be if she could switch off her reactions to him at will. To meet on equal terms, with neither of them caring a rap really what the other one did, would be nice for her peace of mind and a relief to her conscience, which kept warning her that she was getting in over her head and would undoubtedly regret it more than any fleeting pleasure she would have from letting James Foxe get any closer to her.

He sat on the floor beside her, watching her as she split another crumpet and held it out to the flame.

"You'll be kept even busier with me," he said, not without a certain amount of satisfaction. "You won't have time for all these others."

"I'll always have time for my friends!"

He shrugged his shoulders and she could have beaten him over the head with the toasting fork for his indifference.

"I've forgotten the salt," he exclaimed. "I like my crumpets dripping with butter and well salted. Where will I find it?"

She told him, not turning her head in case she forgot her anger with him and allowed him to think she cared what he thought about her. She was herself, and he would either have to accept her as that or go about his own business without her.

She was concentrating so hard on what she was doing that she didn't realise he'd come back into the room until she felt his fingers at the nape of her neck, drawing out the pins that held her hair in place. It fell heavily over her shoulders and he gave a grunt of satisfaction.

"It's more beautiful than ever in the light of the fire," he said.

She did turn and look at him then, her eyes shy. "Don't lose my hairpins, will you? They're expensive and almost impossible to obtain."

He put them neatly on the table beside her battered sofa. "I didn't know they came blond as well as black and brown," he remarked.

"You're not supposed to be able to see them when they're in," she pointed out.

"I prefer them out."

"Evidently," she mocked him. "It wouldn't be very convenient for everyday wear though, would it?"

His smile was intimate and set up a trembling reaction inside her that made it impossible for her to move.

"Long hair brings out the cave man in me. It gives me ideas, like not bothering with these crumpets. We could eat them later . . ."

She blinked, oddly disconcerted. "No, we couldn't. Not after I've been to all this trouble to toast them."

"Wouldn't you rather make love?"

She shook her head, her hair a shimmering cloud about her. "I don't know where you got this idea of me that I leap into bed with every man I meet," she complained. "It isn't true."

He raised his eyebrows in disbelief. "You're just good friends with every one of them?" he enquired dryly.

"Right," she said.

"Aren't you going to make an exception in my case?"

She shook her head again. There was a lump in her throat that refused to go away though she swallowed gamely several times. He made it sound as if she had a choice, and she was beginning to doubt that she had any such thing. The pull of her body and her heart might well prove to be too strong for her will. The latter seemed a poor thing when James Foxe was about. He had already talked her into what amounted to playing truant for the afternoon, into eating crumpets for tea, which she never did because she was always having to watch her weight. And now he expected her to ignore the principles of a lifetime for the fleeting pleasure of being loved by him!

She wanted to, badly, but she wasn't going to admit any such thing to him. She'd be a fool to give him any more power over her than he had already. But it was hard to remember that he was only filling in time with her and it was getting harder by the minute.

He ran his fingers through her hair. "How much are you going to give me? A few kisses?"

She pursed up her lips. "I don't think it would stop there—"

"Not if I can help it! You're beautiful, Sarah, and I want you!"

She pulled away from him, jumping neatly to her feet. "Then you'll have to go on wanting. I'm not in the market for a bit on the side, whatever you may think. There has to be love involved for me."

"I think I could win your heart, Sarah. Will you still deny me then?"

"I'm surprised you want to share me with so many others," she said coolly, though she could feel her pulse flutter.

"I shall insist on exclusive rights, my love. You may kick against it at the beginning, but you'll soon find that pleasing a man of my talents is as much as you can handle and you won't miss those others at all."

She looked at him, envying him his calm confidence. Her green eyes were deep and unfathomable and he cupped her chin, moving her face farther into the light so he could tell what she was thinking.

"You don't believe me?" he accused her.

She brushed his hand away from her face. "I shan't

ever find out! I don't believe you're serious about wanting me anyway. I can't imagine you picking up where some other man has left off."

He was displeased by her frankness and it showed. "You keep telling me there aren't any other men," he retorted with a sharpness that betrayed his anger.

"And you keep telling me you don't believe me!"

His anger changed to amusement. He ran a hand down the full length of her hair and she shivered with an expectation that dismayed her. Anything he did seemed to excite her rebellious body. Why him? Why couldn't it have been someone easy to deal with, like Paul?

"Does that rankle?" he tormented her. "Why is it that the innocent always pretend to be experienced and the other way round? Women are never happy with themselves the way they are."

"You being an expert on women, of course!" she threw back at him.

"Did you think you were the first woman who'd ever attracted me?"

Never! Not for a moment! She was sure there had been many, many others. If she told him she preferred not to think about them, however, he would only laugh at her for being a simpleton. With any luck, he wouldn't guess she was jealous of every one of them, never know that she, who had always taken each day as it came with a lighthearted enjoyment, was vulnerable to every move he made, that she was in danger of having her whole happiness depend on him.

"I won't be the last, either!" she said aloud. Her voice shook a little and she bit into a crumpet as an excuse for her weakness. The butter ran down her chin and, for a moment, she was engrossed in the task of getting the rest of it inside her mouth.

She was unprepared, therefore, when he took the half-eaten crumpet from her fingers and put it back on the plate. His lips closed over hers with a determination she made no effort to resist. She made a little sound of contentment as he gathered her up into his arms, fitting her body to his so that every breath he drew was as close to her as her own. His tongue retrieved the rest of the butter with an intimacy that made her gasp. Then he was kissing her again, exploring her mouth in a way no other man had ever attempted, depriving her of breath altogether.

Perhaps that was why she felt weak and dizzy and wholly unlike her usual self. She ran her hands over his back and shoulders, pleased to find the muscles as hard as if they'd been carved from wood. His hair was pleasant to touch also, clean and springy against her fingers as if it had a life of its own. He leaned back from her, his eyes dark with a passion that was unmistakable in its intensity and that evoked an answering response within her that was quite different from the fleeting excitement she had sometimes felt when Paul had kissed her. This threatened to swallow her whole, leaving her no will of her own, only the ambition to please and be pleased by him.

"You could be what I've been looking for all my life," he said with a ferocity that would have frightened her in other circumstances. "Let me love you, Sarah."

She stared back at him, seeing tiny reflections of herself in the black pupils of his eyes. He must be feeling her need, as she could feel his. It was tearing her apart. She managed a brief shake of her head, shutting her eyes as she did so.

"Love me, and leave me?" she said.

"You could come with me to Holland."

She pushed herself away from him, shaking herself like a puppy coming out of water. How much she would have liked to have given way to him, to take what he offered and let tomorrow take care of itself!

"I can't!" The words were forced out of her as though they hurt her to speak them, which they did.

"Can't, or won't?"

"Both," she said. "I can't throw up my whole way of life for a few days in Holland with you! I have my living to earn. I have my own life and friends to consider. *I'm* not the one miles from base and lonely only until I get back there. That's your problem, not mine!"

"I'm here for at least a year," he pointed out.

"And I hope to live until I'm eighty-five," she replied sardonically.

His eyes narrowed. "You sound as though you're holding out for marriage. Is that it?"

She gave him back look for look. "Would you oblige me if it were?"

"No. I want to be the only man in my wife's life."

Sarah was too miserable even to weep. Her eyes felt like two stones in her head, dry and hard. Why did he always have to come back to this? she wondered dully.

"I think you'd better go," she said.

He had no time to answer. They both heard the scrape of a key in the lock on the front door and watched, with fascinated eyes, as it turned and the door opened. Sarah was frozen into immobility, scared despite herself, for she couldn't think of anyone who had the right to come and go in her place as he pleased.

The door opened a few inches farther and Richard poked his head inside the flat.

"I say, Sarah? Are you there?"

Sarah covered her face with her hands, not uttering a single sound. She heard, but she didn't see, James get to his feet and walk to the door and, in the next moment, Richard was flat on his back on the floor and James was gone.

Chapter Seven

"What does he keep in his fists? Rocks?"

Sarah looked at Richard's purpling jaw and offered an umpteenth apology for her departed guest.

"Did I interrupt anything?" Richard added, his sense of grievance subsiding somewhat.

"Not a lot."

"You looked as though you were having a quarrel, but you don't know him well enough for that, do you?"

How well did you have to know a man to quarrel with him? Sarah didn't really know Richard at all, but she thought she might well end up quarrelling with him over how he had come by her key and why he was using it without her say-so.

"Americans move fast," Sarah contented herself by saying.

Richard tenderly explored his swelling jaw. "I'll say! I never saw him coming at all!"

"He probably thought you were a burglar," Sarah began.

Richard did a double take. "Why should I want to burgle you?"

"Why else are you here?" Sarah asked.

"Me? Your landlady said you were out, but that as I was known to her I could walk up and wait for you. She lent me her key on condition I return it to her on the way out, and I wasn't to keep you up talking until all hours because you worked hard enough at that office of yours and she didn't approve of you seeing clients when you were at home and resting."

Sarah wished James could have heard all that. Perhaps she should have introduced him to Mrs. Vermuyden on the way up. Her landlady was of Dutch descent, as her husband had been, and was the last person to put up with any "goings-on" in her house. She watched over Sarah like a mother hen, her excuse being that Sarah's mother had left her daughter in her care and it was up to her to see Sarah fed herself properly and didn't get into trouble. Trouble, as far as that lady was concerned, meant one thing only: men.

Sarah didn't mind. She had been content to introduce all her friends to Mrs. Vermuyden, male and female, because it had never occurred to her to do otherwise. It was only James Foxe she had kept to herself, because she hadn't wanted Mrs. Vermuyden embarrassing her by giving James one of her lectures on how a nicely brought-up young girl expected to be treated when she was out with a man. Sarah had thought that James, the more so as he was an American, would think her quaintly old-fashioned and might even tell her where she got off. Sarah hadn't wanted him to know that, far from being a flighty piece of his imagination, she had a chaperon watching out for her round every corner and had, so far, never been tempted to put a foot out of line. It was too late to tell him that now, though, when she would probably never see him again.

Richard pulled himself to his feet, groaning under his breath. "Wasn't he the chap who came into your office the day you proved my farm was really mine?"

Sarah nodded. "He comes from Boston in America."

"He seems to have moved in on you quite effectively," Richard complained.

"We didn't know who was coming in."

"Is that a reason to knock my head off? Are all Americans so violent?"

Sarah shrugged her shoulders. "You deserved it, Richard. You could've rung the bell before you used the key."

He winced. "I will in future. I feel a wreck! I've a good mind to go after him and give him a taste of his own medicine."

Sarah didn't bother to answer that. She knew that nothing would induce Richard to face up to James under any circumstances, but if it made him feel better to think he would, why should she disillusion him. She had her own worries to contend with.

"You took us by surprise," Sarah explained yet again. "What did you want with me, anyway?"

"I need another copy of the whole family tree for my lawyer, certified by you as a disinterested party in the dispute. Apparently some old biddy is kicking up because she reckons her son ought to have a half-share in the farm. It does prove that I'm the sole heir, doesn't it?"

Sarah nodded. "You're the only male in the direct line of descent," she affirmed, "so you're the only one who fits the conditions of the entail. It's all yours, Richard. Doesn't your solicitor confirm that?"

"He says this woman means to take it to court. She might know something we don't."

"Call me as a witness," Sarah suggested.

Richard's brow cleared. "I say, may I? You're a brick, Sarah! I'm sorry if I put my foot in it just now."

"More like your chin." Sarah sighed.

"Is there anything I can do to put things right?"

"Nothing." Sarah wished he wouldn't look at her like a labrador who wanted to please but couldn't resist running ahead of the guns. He was a nice man, but she could willingly have wrung his neck for the trouble he'd caused her.

"Oh, well, you've only to say the word and I'll explain everything to your American—"

"What makes you think he'd believe you?"

Richard was first shocked and then so busy rearranging his ideas about Sarah that she would have laughed if she hadn't been so close to tears.

"I say," he said, "have you got something going with him?"

"Not any more," said Sarah.

"Because I let myself in with your landlady's key?"

"You were the last straw," she told him. "He

already thinks I have every man in the place after me.''

"You ought to be flattered! There are a lot of pretty girls in town.''

"Tell that to James! No, on second thought, don't. As he would be the first to point out, that doesn't mean that they all allow themselves to be caught by every man they meet.''

Richard's jaw dropped, making him wince with pain. "Is that what he thinks about you? He must be mad!''

"Thanks," Sarah said dryly.

"But it's obvious to everyone that you—well, you know. I mean, I might have asked you out myself if I'd thought otherwise. I might have asked you anyway if I'd got everything settled and knew what kind of future I have, but I thought Paul had got in first. What does he think of the American?''

"I wish you wouldn't call him that," Sarah said with irritation. "He has a name. He isn't a whole country!''

Richard rubbed his finger against his nose. "It isn't like you to be so touchy," he complained. "He *is* an American!''

"As far as I'm concerned, he's James Foxe!''

Too late, she remembered James's accusation that she thought of him as a category rather than as a person in his own right. If she had, she didn't any longer. To describe him as an American was as inadequate as calling one of her stepfather's Derby winners as a horse like any other. James was . . . James—sometimes known as Jim, though never by her. She liked the name too well to shorten it to anything as mundane as Jim.

"I think I'd better go," Richard said. He gave her a puzzled look. "How did this American—sorry, James Foxe!—get so close to you so quickly? I heard you took him to visit your mother? I didn't believe it at the time. What happened to all those protestations that you never mixed your professional with your personal relationships?"

Sarah could only wonder that herself. "I thought he might be feeling strange on his own in England."

"So you took it upon yourself to introduce him to the natives?"

"Something like that. Actually he has his sister's family stationed at Mildenhall—"

"And he introduced you to her?"

Sarah nodded. She became aware of her hair hanging loose about her shoulders and did it up quickly, pinning it into place with a prim expression on her face. Richard whistled under his breath and she was glad when the movement hurt him. There was little doubt what he was thinking, and Sarah could have kicked him for it. Richard would talk if she didn't successfully head him off by being franker with him than she had intended.

"My mother invited her for tea. My mother is like that. She invites everyone to tea and makes a lot of tiny cucumber sandwiches and has that sort of cake that reminds men of their school days. I didn't even know he had a sister."

"And now he's trying to take advantage of you?"

"No, of course not! He's just being friendly." A blush swept upwards from her neck to her hairline and she wished she'd left well alone. "Well, he did kiss me," she admitted, "but it was my fault as much as it was his."

Richard looked scornful. "Paul'll sort him out for you," he said with a confidence Sarah had never felt in that young man. "No wonder he's been grumbling about the fickleness of women and how you can't trust one of them out of your sight. You should have told him what was happening, Sarah. He's probably imagining all sorts of goings-on."

Sarah almost laughed. With two men looking on her as some sort of scarlet woman, she might even come to believe it herself.

"Why should Paul fight my battles?" she said with a smile. "Forget all about it, Richard. James is here today and gone tomorrow. He can't matter much to any of us."

"If you say so." He relaxed his attitude of bewildered but willing defender and sat down instead. "I can't blame him for kissing you," he added. "Often thought I'd like to myself."

Sarah affected an innocent expression. "Americans are much more forward than we are," she murmured.

"I believe it," Richard affirmed. "You can see it in their films. They never spend any time getting to know each other."

"So," said Sarah, "no harm done? Except to your jaw."

"No. I'm glad I came when I did, though. You ought to look out, Sarah. I can imagine a lot of girls would think him the answer to their prayers. You wouldn't want him to think you were one of them, would you? Can't you get shot of his family tree and get him out of your hair?"

"No," said Sarah, "I can't. It wouldn't be very professional of me, would it? That sort of thing gets about. I make a living out of the Americans and the Australians who can trace their beginnings back to Lincolnshire. I can't afford any gossip about my work."

Richard grinned. "Message understood. I shan't whisper a word, even to Paul. I don't want you to change your mind about appearing as a witness for me. But be careful, Sarah. They speak English like us, but as somebody said, we're two peoples divided by the same language. We don't always mean the same thing by the same words."

"I'll remember," Sarah agreed meekly. She wondered how many Americans Richard had known in his lifetime.

"Met this fellow in a pub once," he went on, more avuncular than ever. "He knew someone who'd been over there and bought himself an American car—a gas-guzzler, he called it. They call petrol gas, you know, short for gasoline. Well, anyway, there's a lot in looking at a chap's car if you want to know what a man is like. Doesn't work with women, but it does with a man. This man told me that, and there's a lot in it. Americans drive big cars and we don't. That must mean something. You think about it."

"I will," Sarah promised him.

Richard gave her a shrewd look that told her he knew exactly what she was thinking. "You can laugh at me all you like, but have a long, quiet look at his car sometime and you'll see what I mean."

"He drives a Mercedes over here," she told him.

"He must be making a lot of money."

"He's a lawyer. I think he's attached to the International Court at The Hague."

"He's not a judge, is he?"

Sarah gulped. "I don't think so. He isn't old enough to be a judge!"

"Not here," Richard agreed. "They're mostly in their dotage by the time they're appointed to the bench over here, but they're elected over there. Don't you remember seeing that film? What was it called? There was this young lawyer trying to get elected into office to clean up the town—"

"A district attorney isn't a judge," Sarah objected.

They looked at each other in mutual bafflement. "Ask him what he is," Richard directed her. "It would be something if he were a judge, wouldn't it?"

Sarah supposed that it would be. She rather hoped he wasn't anything as exalted as a judge, however. She didn't want to think of him in any other way than the man who had taken her into his arms and had kissed her. A judge wouldn't have socked another man on the jaw without listening to and weighing up the evidence first. Judges were careful men who had left the wild ways of youth far behind them. They weren't unruly, passionate, and jealous—

Was that what had been the matter with James? Had he been jealous? Sarah's heart leaped within her. Jealousy implied more feeling than she had thought he had for her. For a moment she allowed herself to hope, but then reality returned and she knew it wasn't because of any emotion he felt for her. It was far more likely to that he was unreasonably territorial and didn't like anyone tresspassing. She knew the type. Even weak, fussy Paul felt the same way though he never acted upon it.

Richard looked rather wistful as he turned to say good night to her at the door.

"If you're ever free, Sarah, I meant what I said about taking you out. Will you let me know?"

She shut the door behind him, wishing she could have fallen for someone as simple and as uncomplicated as Richard, who would make few demands and who didn't suspect her of carrying on with every male around.

It was a long time before she slept that night. She spent the small hours trying to think of a way to convince James how wrong he was about her, but every time she came up with a more or less convincing solution she remembered that he probably wasn't coming back. And what a good thing that was—she was better off without him, living her own life in peace.

It was a miserable week. The weather, reflecting her mood, was damp and dark, and she felt like a mole, having to use the electric light even in the middle of the day. On Tuesday, Sarah forced herself to join in with the usual group, but the new song she had written for them wasn't well received and Paul was at his most difficult.

"For heaven's sake, Sarah," he had muttered on their way home. "What's got into you? Nobody wants to sing a dirge at this time of year. We'd have been better off practising those carols you want us to sing this Christmas."

"I thought you weren't coming carol-singing," Sarah answered him.

"Anything's better than seeing you moping about like this. It's all to do with that American, isn't it?"

"No, it isn't!" She didn't know which annoyed her most, to be accused of being a blight, or to hear James described as "that American." She was getting everything out of perspective, and it was getting worse, not better. Even when she was asleep she couldn't escape her misery over James. He haunted her dreams, waking and sleeping. If he were to ask her now to go with him to Holland it would be a very different story.

"Then what is it to do with?" Paul demanded, reasonably enough.

"I don't know! It's probably the time of year."

But it wasn't the time of year that disturbed her working day later on in the week. She came into her office after a briefly snatched lunch that she was sure was going to give her indigestion all afternoon, and there, waiting for her, was Mary Beth. Sarah tried to pretend she wasn't flustered by her unexpected presence. She sat down at her desk with a calmness she was far from feeling and, when she could delay no longer, looked up at James's sister.

"I hope you haven't been waiting long," she said.

"I'd have waited all day, if necessary," Mary Beth answered cheerfully. "I had to see you."

"Yes?" Sarah said carefully. "If it's about that plaque in the church at Heckington—"

"Gracious no! It's about Jim. What have you done to him?"

Sarah's face closed down. "I wasn't aware I'd done anything. It was he who did the doing. He knocked a friend of mine flat on his back. He was lucky Richard didn't sue him for assault and battery."

"Oh, dear," said Mary Beth, on the point of laughter.

"It wasn't funny!"

Mary Beth sobered. "No, I don't suppose it was. Poor Jim! You won't tell him I came to see you—at least not about him, will you?"

"I don't suppose I'll have the opportunity."

"Bad as that? Louise was so smarmy yesterday I wondered if she knew something I didn't. She said Jim wouldn't be going to Boston any more. I took it to be wishful thinking on her part. But why? You were getting along so well together."

The knowledge that James had discussed her with Louise knocked most of the stuffing out of Sarah. She felt physically ill that he could have betrayed their friendship in that way. She wouldn't have minded his telling Mary Beth, but Louise she had disliked on sight and she was sure he'd known it.

"I don't think I was ever more than a potential bit on the side," she told Mary Beth wryly. "He'll be going home to Louise—or someone—eventually."

Mary Beth was already shaking her head. "I can see he didn't tell you why he came over here in the first place. He doesn't much like these international cases and he wouldn't have taken it, even though it concerned a friend of his, if he hadn't wanted to get away from home for a while. His girl married somebody else. She never said a word to him, accepted his ring, agreed to a date, everything! And then, pow! She sent a note round saying she was sorry, she'd married someone else. Jim thought he was in love with her and it was horrible for him. He came away until the worst of the gossip died down."

"Oh," said Sarah. "I'm sorry, but I don't see what it has to do with me."

Mary Beth gave her a look that was very like her brother's. "I could shake you, Sarah Gilbert! Of course it has to do with you! Do you want Louise to have him?"

"If that's what he wants."

"He doesn't! He wants you!"

Sarah leaned back in her chair, overwhelmingly tired. A headache was beginning behind her eyes and, much as she liked Mary Beth, she wished heartily she'd go away and leave her alone.

"He wants me for a brief affair, no more than that. He probably wants to get the bad taste out of his mouth before he goes off to pastures new." She held up a hand as Mary Beth prepared to break in. "No, hear me out, please. He never pretended to want anything else. You see, when he first saw me he decided it was the kind of thing I went in for and, no matter what I said, he went right on believing it. Richard was the last straw."

"He's a fool!" his sister said. "Anyone could see you're not like that!" She eyed Sarah thoughtfully, her brow creased with a new anxiety. "On second thought, perhaps it isn't so surprising. He took quite a toss over Jenny, and none of us thought *she* was carrying on with anyone else either."

Sarah raised her chin defiantly. "It doesn't matter to me what he thinks. If I were interested, I shouldn't want to catch anyone on the rebound. The only reason for getting married, in my opinion, is because one can do no other."

"Oh, my dear, how much I agree with you!" Mary Beth said with approval. "It was like that for Pete and me. I'm miserable when we're separated, even for a few days. It wasn't like that with Jim and Jenny, though. At least, I don't think it was. She was far too interested in his career for me to quite like her. I think that was her interest in Jim at that, because the other man is ordained in some church or other, and ministers of religion don't usually make much money, not unless they have their own TV channel. If anyone can get it for him, it'll be Jenny. You don't have these little local stations over here, do you?"

Sarah shook her head. She didn't want to hear anything more about Jenny. The mention of her name as someone James had thought he was in love with had been enough to tie her innards in knots, and there was no denying this time that it was sheer jealousy that was making her feel that way.

"I'm glad you came," she said, her voice even, almost as though she didn't care at all. "I'll need to know what to do with your family tree. If James isn't coming back, shall I send it to you when I've finished it, or shall I send it directly to your mother?"

"What makes you think James won't be back?" Mary Beth demanded.

"He's nothing to come back for," Sarah said simply.

"You mean you won't see him if he does?"

"He won't want to come back."

"Oh, yes he will, when he's gotten over whatever it was you quarrelled about. You're good for him, Sarah. You're the first girl he's ever looked at whom I've really liked!"

Sarah smiled a thin smile. "Much James would care for that! Now, if you'll give me your mother's address—"

"No, I won't. You can come over to Mildenhall and deliver it personally. Pete and I'd love to have you for a weekend—whatever you can spare—and be blowed to that brother of mine!"

Sarah thought she might like that, if Mary Beth could guarantee that James wouldn't be there. Of course, if she really wanted to cut James right out of her life it was foolish to befriend his sister. She wasn't sure what to do.

"Think about it," encouraged Mary Beth. She rose to her feet with the unconscious elegance of one who always looked good in whatever she wore. "By the way," she said, "Jim will skin me alive if he thinks I've been interfering in his affairs—" She hesitated. "Oops, sorry, perhaps I should have said his life? He knows I had it planned to come to Boston some time anyway, though. What should I see while I'm here, so he'll know it isn't a blind for seeing you?"

Sarah stood up also. "The Guild Hall. I'll walk over there with you."

"You don't have to," Mary Beth protested.

"I want to," Sarah said.

It was Wednesday, and the marketplace was filled with stalls selling every conceivable object. It took the two women a long time to make their way down the

aisles and on to where the Guild Hall nestled, next
door to Fydell House, the most distinguished town-
house in Boston, now the home of Pilgrim College
and the property of the Boston Preservation Trust.
Inside there was a room opened by John F. Kennedy's
father when he was the United States Ambassador to
the Court of St. James, in recognition of the money
which has poured across the Atlantic to the benefit of
the American Boston's mother town in England.

Sarah tried to give Mary Beth some idea of the
history of the Guild Hall as they made their way down
South Street. The pavements were narrow, however,
and every few seconds Mary Beth would stop to
exclaim over another of the medieval buildings that
lined the street.

"It belonged to the Guild of the Blessed Mary?
Who were they when they were at home?"

"In the Middle Ages people often grouped themselves together for both religious and secular reasons.
The Guild of the Blessed Mary was the oldest and the
richest in Boston. But that isn't why I brought you
here. It has a connection with the Pilgrim Fathers
too."

"Before the Boston influx?"

"Oh, yes, the real Pilgrim Fathers were imprisoned
here when they tried to escape to Holland. They were
betrayed by the captain of the ship they'd hired to take
them across the North Sea. In those days, the twin
rulers were the monarch and the Church. Elizabeth
felt obliged to have a go at the Puritans because they
kept fulminating against the established church, and
that was a danger to the whole state. She said she

'made no windows into men's souls, meaning they could think what they liked as long as they didn't publish it abroad. But nothing would stop the Puritans! They thought the Anglican bishops were too much like the Catholic ones they'd suffered under when Elizabeth's sister Mary was on the throne. They couldn't and wouldn't compromise, which was the whole essence of the Church of England."

"What brought them here?"

"Boston was one of the great ports of England in those days, and Holland was a protestant country. Their leader, William Brewster, brought the Fathers here the year before Elizabeth died in 1602. You can see the cells where they were held pending being sent away to Lincoln for trial. They tried to get to Holland again later and were successful."

Mary Beth was intrigued by the tiny cells where the Pilgrim Fathers had been held. She walked in and out of them several times, sitting on the single wooden bench and imagining what it had felt like, crowded together in such a small space.

"I'd have given up and gone home after a spell in here," she avowed. "Will they mind if I take a few pictures for Mom? She adores this sort of thing."

"Help yourself," Sarah invited her.

It was getting dark when Mary Beth finally decided she really would have to be getting back to Mildenhall.

"Shall I tell Jim that I saw you?" she said as she got into her Lincoln with a wry smile at the narrow entrance to the car park.

"No, please don't," said Sarah. "Don't tell him

anything at all. If he wants to know, he knows where to find me. Good-bye, Mary Beth. Drive carefully!"

Mary Beth reached out of the window and kissed Sarah on the cheek. "Don't forget, you're coming to stay with Pete and me at Mildenhall. Keep in touch, Sarah. I'll never forgive you if you don't!"

Chapter Eight

The bell pealed urgently, desisted for a while, and then pealed again. Sarah turned over reluctantly in bed, wondering who on earth could be at the door at that hour of the morning. A glance at her watch confirmed that it was little more than six o'clock. It was Friday, a working day, and she expected no one.

With even greater reluctance than she had brought to waking, she slid her feet out of bed and reached for her dressing gown, which was warm if not glamorous. The day hadn't even dawned as she opened her door and flopped her way down the stairs to the main door, which Mrs. Vermuyden kept locked and barred after midnight.

"Who is it?"

The only answer was another ring at the bell. Sarah forced the bolt back with some difficulty. It was old and rusty and she always had difficulty with it. She opened the door a crack and repeated her question. "Who's there?"

The door was forced open against her protesting body and James Foxe stepped inside, closing the door behind him.

"Upstairs with you!" he commanded. "We'll have your landlady out to see what we're doing if you don't hurry up."

The threat was enough for Sarah. She had no wish to face the older woman at this hour, with a man calling on her and herself still in her nightclothes, and with no hope at all of pushing James back out the door.

"What do you want?" she demanded in a forceful whisper.

"You!"

He set off up the stairs at an alarming pace, with her following more slowly in his wake. At six o'clock in the morning! He had to be joking!

By the time she'd gained her small flat, he was already in the kitchen, whistling under his breath as he put the kettle on.

"What do you think you're doing?" she said from the doorway.

He turned and grinned at her. "Getting you some breakfast. Get dressed, love, and then we'll talk. Tea or coffee, by the way?"

"Coffee."

"Good, that's my preference also."

"I don't particularly want anything at this hour of the morning," she said.

He remained abominably cheerful. "Had a late

night? Never mind, you can make it up tonight when you can go to bed as early as you like."

"I don't know what you're talking about. Mrs. Vermuyden—"

"Get dressed, Sarah! I'm not talking to you until I can be sure you're in a fit state to take in what I'm saying."

"Oh, all right!"

She flounced into her bedroom, not quite sure what she was in such a rage about. Oh, but she was glad to see him, no matter what the hour of the morning! She had persuaded herself in these last two days that she would never see him again and that her best course was to root all memory of him out of her being. So far it had been a hopeless task.

She didn't know what to put on. She opened the cupboard she had converted into a wardrobe and stared at its contents, none of which pleased her at that moment. In the end she chose a pants suit—she had only worn it once before—in a gorgeous shade that was a cross between pink and beige. With it she wore a frilly shirt that had flounced sleeves that were madly impractical for everyday wear; but this, as she kept reminding herself, was not an ordinary day.

She was putting the last touches to her makeup when James appeared in her doorway unannounced. The sight of him rendered her breathless and she went on with what she was doing to give herself time to recover her equanimity.

"I was hoping to be in time to see you put up your hair," he said.

She glanced at him in the mirror, shaking her head.

"Don't you think an apology would be in order?" she countered.

"I came early because I didn't want to miss you."

She finished with her powder puff, throwing it down on top of the dressing table, and stood up.

"That wasn't what I was talking about, and you know it. Maybe we're just less violent over here, but we don't go round knocking people down with no reason. You could've broken Richard's jaw!"

"As long as he got the point that he isn't welcome anywhere near you," James said cheerfully, "I'll forgive him his past trespasses."

Sarah said, "Will you indeed? That's big of you."

"I'm in a magnanimous mood—"

"What about Richard's mood?"

"He'll get over losing you in time," James assured her, still cheerful.

"He never had me!" she snapped.

"That's what we're going to talk about as soon as you've had your breakfast. You're looking very beautiful for one who's as prickly as a hedgehog. Feel like kissing me good morning?"

What harm could a single embrace do? None that she could see. Her expression softened as she regarded him, thinking that she could never be angry with him for long. It was so delightful to have him there that she could think of nothing else, not even his motives in coming back to her and at such a ridiculous hour of the morning.

"Mmm," she said, refusing to commit herself.

He took that to be consent and advanced right into her bedroom, looking round with interest at the bed she had hastily pulled together and the simple furnishings which had been all she could afford when she had first taken the flat.

"You have a single bed," he commented. He seemed pleased by the discovery.

His arms slipped about her and she shivered in anticipation of a closer contact. James gave a grunt of satisfaction and she wondered what he was thinking. His hand was already at the ruffles of her shirt, but then he changed his mind.

"This isn't the time for more than a kiss," he said reluctantly, "but it's nice to know that you wouldn't mind including me in the magic circle of your admirers. Soon it's going to be a magic circle of just the two of us. That's what I came to tell you this morning."

"If I knew what you were talking about—" she began.

"After breakfast!"

His arms tightened about her and her whirling thoughts took on a more intimate aspect. He was newly shaved and the tang of whatever it was that he had put on afterwards was pleasant in her nostrils. She ran her fingers through the hair at the nape of his neck and pulled his head closer to her own, her mouth more than ready for the assault of his.

When he broke the embrace the sensation of loss brought the tears into her eyes and she blinked them back hastily, smiling wryly at her own reactions to this man she could no longer think of as an American and a foreigner.

"Come on," he said. "The coffee will be cold if we dally in here any longer."

He made coffee stronger than she did, probably because he hadn't followed the frequent price rises, one by one, until she'd begun to wonder if she could afford to drink as much of it as she did. It was very good, better than she remembered her usual brand to be. He smiled at her expression, spreading his hands to acknowledge his guilt.

"It's my sister's coffee. She buys it in the PX, real American coffee that you can taste! Much of the stuff you get in England needs a label on it to tell you what you're supposed to be drinking."

Sarah laughed in the back of her throat. "This is nectar," she agreed.

"I brought some other goodies with me," he said. "We've got English muffins, eggs and bacon for breakfast. Why can't one get English muffins in England?"

"One can," Sarah insisted, though it was a long time since they'd appeared in any of the shops she patronized. "We eat them for tea at four o'clock in the afternoon."

"Does that mean you'd rather have had pancakes and maple syrup with your eggs and bacon?" he asked her.

She shuddered at the thought. "No."

He frowned. "What do you usually have?"

"Toast and marmalade, if I bother with anything at all."

"Never mind," he said, "you'll get used to having a proper breakfast with me. I'm a great believer in starting the day right, and then it doesn't matter what happens the rest of the day."

She gave him a thoughtful look over the rim of her cup. "With you?" she repeated.

He nodded in a businesslike fashion. "I was pretty angry the other night."

"I gathered that," she said dryly.

"It's a long story," he went on, "which I'm not going to bore you with, but it made me think I'd be a fool to have anything more to do with you. I didn't want any more pain of that sort. I'd been fooling myself that I could make you want me and only me, that you weren't as susceptible as the rest of your sex to anything in pants. I hadn't reckoned with my own need for you. I've been pretty busy these last few days, but the nights were my own and after living through a couple of them I decided this wasn't like last time and that I was going to have to do something about it. If I can't put up with you the way you are and I can't do without you either, I was going to have to change something. Are you with me so far?"

"Faint but pursuing," Sarah answered.

It was obvious he thought her response flippant and was annoyed by it. 'It's no laughing matter!" he growled.

"No, it isn't," she agreed, suddenly as grave as even he could have wished. The import of what he'd told her was only just sinking in, and she didn't like the look of it at all. What did he mean that she was susceptible to anything in pants? He'd thought her promiscuous all along, but this seemed one stage worse. Didn't he think she had any discrimination at all?

She felt cold all over. She had made matters worse by responding so eagerly to him every time he kissed her, she thought with a sinking feeling in her breast, but she was no more able to hide the attraction he had for her than flap her arms in the air and fly. Why, oh why, should he think that she was as eager for every man's embrace as she was for his? What had she ever done to deserve his opinion of her?

"You'll be happy with me," he said at last.

It was a simple, devastating statement, the truth of which sent all other considerations tumbling from her mind. Mechanically, she bit into one of the muffins he had prepared and found it full of a mixture of bacon and egg that crumbled as she ate it, spilling out of the corners of her mouth. It was very good.

"Perhaps you'd better tell me exactly why you're here," she invited him. "You do realise this is an ordinary working day as far as I'm concerned? I have several appointments this morning—"

"You'll have to cancel them."

"Oh?" She looked down her nose, finding a crumb on her upper lip. "I have my living to earn. I have to have a very good reason before I start taking days off."

He leaned forward until they were almost touching. "Sarah, I'm taking you away. I've thought about this all week. If I can't change you and I can't change the way I feel about you, the only thing I can change is the way you live."

"I'm very happy with the way I live!"

His mouth tightened into a stubborn line. "You *think* you are!"

"I am. I am!"

"I'm surprised your landlady puts up with it," he went on, getting back into his stride. "If you don't come willingly, I'll tell her a thing or two and she'll put you out the door. I'm sure it's against the house rules to have men in your room all night."

She raised her chin in indignation. "What men? Are you going to tell her you've been here all night?"

His eyes dropped before hers. "It won't do any good getting angry, Sarah. You're coming with me until I've proved to you how much better your life'll be with only one man to worry about."

She stared at him, unable to believe her ears. "You're going to reform me!" She still couldn't believe it, even when he nodded his assent. A giggle broke in the back of her throat and she choked over it. "I'm afraid I'm going to be a terrible disappointment to you!" she exclaimed as he kindly thumped her on the back.

"You'll never be that! A trifle unexpected sometimes, but never disappointing. What else am I to do about you, woman? If I can't do without you, I have to convert you to my way of thinking."

"You could ask me," she suggested, the tears pouring down her cheeks as she recovered herself from the choking fit.

He brushed away her tears, his fingers lingering against her skin. "You don't need the Pauls and Richards of this world, but you won't believe me until I can prove to you otherwise. You'll get all the loving you need from me—"

"Until you go back to America? Or until you've got me out of your system?"

His jaw clenched. "The only thing that'll destroy it will be if you start playing around with someone else."

"Which I'm bound to do as soon as you let me out of your sight?"

His fingers stiffened, taking a firm hold on the lobe of her ear. "I won't be letting you out of my sight until I've convinced you you need me as much as I need you!"

She pulled her head away, her eyes blurring with an unexpected emotion that she barely recognised. It was ridiculous that he should be going to so much trouble to combat what was nothing more than a figment of his imagination, but she was touched that he should be so determined to change her. Jenny, if Mary Beth was to be believed, had been given no such second chance.

"I see," Sarah said aloud. "Where are you taking me? Or are you planning to move in here with me?"

"With all your other friends walking in and out at will?"

She recovered her sense of humour along with her breath after her fit of choking, and when she looked at him there was a distinct twinkle in her eyes. "That might be awkward," she admitted slowly, "though it depends what you mean to do with me when you've got me. Are we going to a hotel? I may as well tell you now that I never use a name which isn't my own!"

He glowered back at her. "No, we're not going to a hotel!"

She allowed herself the tiniest of smiles. "I'm glad of that. Hotels of that kind are so sordid, don't you think?"

He shrugged his shoulders indifferently.

"You're taking me to Mary Beth!" she exclaimed. Relief flooded through her.

"To Mary Beth?" He laughed shortly. "She'd mount shotgun over you all night!"

Sarah's glance mocked him. "You mean she doesn't think I need saving from myself?"

"She doesn't know you; I do!"

"Not well enough," she said. "Where are we going? To Holland?"

He refused to answer. Instead he poured her out another cup of coffee, adding some milk and pushing the sugar bowl towards her.

"Drink that," he commanded, "and then pack what you'll need for a weekend. Oh, and you'd better write a note to pin on your office door in case you can't get hold of any of your appointments to put them off."

"What shall I tell them?" she asked him sweetly. "That I've been carried off by you to your temporary cave?"

"Many a true word is spoken in jest," he retorted. "It may not be as temporary as you hope, but the caveman bit—"

"Are you going to *carry* me down the stairs?" she suggested hopefully.

"No, I'm not! I'm going to drag you down them by the hair on your head!"

She laughed. "That'll be interesting for Mrs. Vermuyden." Draining the last of her coffee, she put the cup down on the table. "I'll go and pack. What will I need? Warm and comfortable, or smart and with it?"

"Warm and comfortable. I'm not sure about the heating at this place."

Her face was sober, but her eyes laughed at him "There will be a roof over our heads, I trust?"

"Oh, yes. And walls. There's even a laid-on water supply."

"Then what's wrong with it?"

"Well, the potential is greater than the actuality at the moment. When it's been done up it's going to be just fine."

Sarah didn't ask any more questions. She was well used to packing for a weekend; it was second nature to her to keep a sponge bag at the ready for when she went home to her mother's every other weekend. In a matter of moments she had found the few pieces of thermal underwear she had bought in the foul winter of a couple of years before and had put out her warmest sweaters, together with some old paint-stained trousers and a skirt of which she was not too ashamed, in case it was needed. She slipped the lot into the soft bag she could sling over her shoulder and went back to the sitting room, where James was waiting for her.

"You can wash up while I ring my clients," she ordered him.

He looked blank for a moment. "You mean wash the dishes?" he checked with her.

"What else could I mean?"

"I'll have to try to remember that we wash up before a meal and you after it," he said smiling.

Everyone was very understanding that she was obliged to take the day off. She felt a bit of a fraud as she juggled her diary round to accommodate them the following week, putting one or two of them to consid-erable trouble to fit in with her change of dates. She had to be out of her mind to take the day off at the busiest time of her year. James, she thought, had a lot to answer for, and she opened her mouth to tell him so, changing her mind when she realised that he'd finished doing the dishes and was standing uncomfortably just behind her, listening to her excuses.

"Will you lose a lot of money over this?" he asked her.

"Not too bad. Do you care?"

"I'd offer to make it up to you, but I don't suppose you'd take it."

"No, I wouldn't." She checked her appointments one last time to make sure she hadn't overlooked anyone, then looked up at him, her eyes wide and very green. "What would that make me if I allowed you to pay me?"

"Sarah, it isn't like that!"

"Then tell me how it is?"

"I tried it without you, but I won't share you with anyone else. I have to prove it to you that you'll be happy with only me for company!"

"All right. Prove it to me," she said.

He was disconcerted, but he hadn't changed his mind. "Is that all you're taking with you?" he asked.

"I'll leave a note for Mrs. Vermuyden and then I'm ready," she announced, scribbling a few words on the pad by the telephone. "Are we going by car?"

He nodded. "Mine, not yours. We'll be uncomfortable enough when we get there."

She didn't mind his casting aspersions on her car. It served her well, and that was all that mattered to her. On the other hand, to be driven in his Mercedes was a novelty that verged on the luxurious. There weren't many people who were averse to first-class travel if they could get it. It wasn't necessary to her, but she intended to enjoy every minute of it.

He went down the stairs first, leaving her to lock her front door and slip the note she had written through Mrs. Vermuyden's on the ground floor. By the time she joined him, he had unlocked the doors of the Mercedes and had put her bag on the back seat beside his. She got silently into the passenger seat and fastened her belt, revelling in the ease at which it clicked into place—another difference from the twisted pieces of black cloth that graced her much older vehicle.

"Are you going to tell me now where we're going?" she asked as he got in beside her.

He grinned. "Not yet," he said. "I can't afford to have you running out on me now."

She had no intention of running anywhere, but she could hardly tell him that. "I think I may be able to stand your society for one weekend," she said.

"Without pining for your other friends?"

She sighed, trying not to let her annoyance at the question show. There was a long silence, and then she said, "I'm not Jenny, James. I'm me, Sarah Gilbert, remember?"

Chapter Nine

The silence was something tangible that stretched between them until Sarah began to think it would be impossible to break it. There'd be nothing but silence for ever and ever, with the two of them carefully not touching and avoiding each other's eyes as if even that fragile contact would be too much to be borne.

"What do you know about Jenny?"

The question was shot at her without James apparently speaking at all. Sarah shuffled in her seat and wondered what she should answer. "I know you were engaged to be married to her," she said at last. "And that she married somebody else. I'm sorry."

"What have you got to be sorry about? Don't you like taking on someone another woman's scorned?"

"I think she was a fool," Sarah said slowly and clearly.

"Who told you? Mary Beth? She never has learned to mind her own business."

"She cares about you," Sarah pointed out. "You're lucky to have a family that cares."

"Doesn't yours?"

"Of course, but I know plenty who don't. Paul never sees his parents from one year's end to the other, not even at Christmas. They went abroad last year, and the year before that there was some other excuse—"

"I don't wish to hear about Paul!"

Sarah gave him an exasperated look. "And I don't care to be bracketed with Jenny! That makes us quits!"

"You don't know anything about Jenny—"

"I know you thought you were in love with her!"

"I'd have married her if she hadn't—hadn't—"

"Married somebody else? It was better before than after. Perhaps you didn't make it easy for her to tell you that she'd fallen for someone else. You can be pretty intimidating when you want to be."

"Women are all the same! You'd let one man make love to you and go blithely off with another, wouldn't you?"

"I never have," she said.

"Then what are you doing with me now?"

"I didn't realise I had any choice—"

"You don't think I'd really have dragged you down the stairs by your hair!" he cut in.

"No. I wouldn't have come if I hadn't wanted to. I'm not engaged to be married to another man, however."

"What other promises have you made to Paul, or Richard, or both of them?"

"I've never promised anything to any man."

His scornful look condemned her as a liar. "Do you give without making any promises? That'll suit me very well!"

Sarah looked down at her hands and saw that they were shaking. If he hadn't sounded so hurt she could have hated James for doing this to her.

"I've come with you," she whispered. "Isn't that enough for you? Do you have to spoil it all for me? I'd have preferred it to have meant something to you too, but I suppose Jenny meant too much to you—"

"Jenny didn't mean a thing!"

She was confused. "You were going to marry her. She must have meant something to you."

"She was suitable and she would have been good for my career."

"That's what you're telling yourself now," Sarah said as calmly as she could, "but it wasn't like that at the time. Mary Beth said you were very much in love with her."

"Mary Beth can't imagine anyone getting married unless they were head over heels in love," he pointed out dryly. "That was one of the reasons she couldn't get along with Jenny. Where Mary Beth has stars in her eyes, the Jennys of this world have dollar signs."

In which category did he place her? "I'm with Mary Beth," Sarah said firmly, in case there should be any doubt in the matter.

"At least you sometimes think of something other than money," he agreed.

The silence grew between them again until Sarah burst out, "Didn't you miss Jenny at all?"

"I felt guilty for a while," he said. "I missed you more when I was away from you last week."

That was better still! "I missed you too," she said.

She didn't mind the silence after that. She began to take an interest in where they were going, and decided they were going towards Cambridge. The black earth of the fens had been newly ploughed and the lights in the sky were vivid, lighting up every corner of the fields and the strips of water that drained and divided them. Flocks of migrating birds swirled overhead, chattering in sharp discord as they found their places in the first dancing flights that got them ready for the longer flight across the North Sea to the continent and beyond.

They stopped short of Cambridge, however. James turned off the road they were on for one narrower still. He glanced across at her and she was glad to see his mood had lightened considerably in the last hour.

"I bought this cottage when you wouldn't come to Holland with me last weekend. It needs rather a lot doing to it."

"You *bought* it! But it takes weeks to buy a house! Surely you haven't got the key already?"

"I've had it a couple of days. I bought the place lock, stock and barrel, furniture and all. The owner agreed I could rent it until all the formalities are completed. It has an old-fashioned garden, the kind one associates with England."

"And dry rot in the roof?" she finished for him.

"It has beetle in the floor," he replied with dignity. "Someone is coming tomorrow to deal with it. Otherwise all it needs is a coat of paint and a bit of polish. You'll like it!"

Sarah did like it. She more than liked it; it was exactly the sort of house she had one day dreamed of owning. It was full of oak beams, but one wasn't in constant danger of decapitation as was so often the case with medieval and Tudor houses. This house had a pedigree that proclaimed it had once been owned by someone of importance. It meant that the rooms were reasonably spacious and that the windows were large, welcoming light into the dingily painted interiors. Some of the lights had stained glass in them, and some of them were so old that one could hardly see through the glass at all.

"Look at those floorboards!" she exclaimed. "They must measure a foot across at least!"

"I knew you'd like it," James said. "Come upstairs and I'll show you where you'll be sleeping."

She hung back for the barest moment, then thought that if he could go through with it so could she. There was no point displaying her lack of experience in carrying off these occasions if he didn't believe in it anyway. There would be time enough for that later. Right now she knew there was one man she wanted in her life more than any other and she was willing to pay the price of keeping him there for as long as possible. She couldn't imagine there would ever be anybody else she'd sooner have initiate her into the mysteries of womanhood. She was very much in love with James Foxe and, having acquired a reasonable knowledge of herself in her growing-up years, she was sure she'd never love another man in quite the same way.

The room was the only one to have been redecorated. James told her proudly he had done it himself, trying to paint her out of his system.

"I was standing here when I realised I couldn't do it," he added, not quite looking at her. "You were here in the room with me. I kept thinking, she'll like this colour, or those drapes won't do anything for her. I even moved all the furniture round. I could see you in front of this vanity, the other has nowhere for you to keep your hairpins, or your other bits and bobs. Do you like it?"

"I love it!" Sarah said.

She held out her arms to him, touched beyond measure that he should make such a confession. She had almost said she loved him, but that would never do. He wasn't ready for that, not by a long way, if he ever would be. For a moment she thought he was going to refuse her silent invitation, but then she was lifted clear off her feet into his arms as he whirled her about the room. The floor creaked ominously and he put her down hastily. But he didn't let go. He held her tightly against him as if he still couldn't quite believe she was really there.

"How long did Richard stay with you the other night?" he demanded hoarsely.

"Half an hour. He'd have been gone sooner if you hadn't almost broken his jaw."

"What did he want?"

"He wanted me to appear as a witness if there's a court case over the land he's farming. There's no doubt he's the real heir, but his cousins choose not to realise it. Lincolnshire land is very valuable."

"He had a key!"

"It wasn't given to him by me. Mrs. Vermuyden thought I was out and told him he could wait for me to come back. Richard has never been my lover and he never will be."

"You like him well enough!"

"I like a lot of people. That doesn't mean I go to bed with them!"

James's arms tightened about her. "Don't talk about it," he ordered her gruffly. "I don't want to hear about the others, past or future. I want to pretend that you're mine and nobody else's!"

Sarah smoothed the rough skin of his face over the bone structure beneath. She was amused to discover that although it was only a few hours since he had shaved, his beard rasped beneath her fingers.

"You don't have to pretend," she said softly. "I'm here, aren't I?"

His kiss was a revelation to her. He held her quite gently, yet she knew there was no gainsaying the barrier of his arms about her. It was pleasant, she discovered, to be helpless for once, to know that his strength was as necessary to the mixture as her response. She opened her mouth to his and arched her body against his in increasing delight. She was hardly aware when he eased her jacket off her shoulders, and when his hand found her breasts she didn't even wonder what had happened to the rest of her clothing. She wanted to make the same discoveries about him. Her fingers found the buttons of his shirt and she flattened her palms against his hair-roughened chest, marveling at how different a man's body felt from her own.

She felt only loss when he released her. He took a
step away from her, his eyes never leaving the curves
of her body which were revealed to his ardent gaze.
To her surprise, she wasn't in the least embarrassed. It
felt right to be there with him, no matter what the
circumstances.

"We have work to do," he said at last, turning away
from her. "Put on some old clothes and we'll start to
make the downstairs habitable. You won't think much
of staying on here if we leave it as it is."

Her heart was thumping against her ribs, but she
said nothing. Her instincts were to tempt him then
and there, but she didn't want to do anything to
confirm his impression of her as a promiscuous
woman. She sat on the edge of the bed, holding the
edges of her shirt together until the weakness of
passion left her limbs and she was able to search in her
bag for the paint-stained clothes she had brought with
her.

"Where are we going to start?" she asked him.

"I thought the kitchen. Better to do the living room
after the beetle has been coped with and that won't be
until I next get back from The Hague." He looked at
her more closely, studying her white face this time.
"Are you all right?"

"I'm fine," she confirmed.

"I hope so," he said, "there's a lot to do."

It took all her resolution to be as matter-of-fact as
he was. She changed her clothes, trying not to mind
that he made no effort to leave her on her own while
she did so. She wasn't used to having anyone in her
bedroom while she dressed. The fact that it was James

made her fingers all thumbs, and even pulling her sweater over her head was an effort that left her breathless and weak at the knees.

She reached up to confirm that her bun was still in place at the nape of her neck and then managed a shaky smile for James. "Right, I'm ready," she said, hoping she didn't sound as shy of him as she felt.

"Pity," he remarked. "I like to see you doing up your hair. One of these days I'll have your portrait painted like that. It must be the most graceful movement known to woman."

The hot colour washed up her neck and into her cheeks. "One of these days?" she mocked him. The words caught in the back of her throat and she stood up abruptly, leading the way out onto the landing and down the creaking wooden stairs to the main hallway.

He caught up with her as she found her way into the kitchen, his hand reaching out for her and fielding her against the hard wall of his chest. He turned her to face him, his finger brushing her still reddened cheek.

"Don't your other admirers pay you any compliments? You blush like a girl who'd never been near a man."

"Perhaps that's what I am," she said.

"If I thought that you wouldn't be here!"

She looked an enquiry, her eyes wide and very green. What difference would it make? she wondered.

"If I thought that, I'd woo you in a very different way, my love. I'd fill your arms with roses and invite you to my sister's for Thanksgiving, giving you all the time you need to fall in love with me. As it is, I'm going to make your need for me blot out what any other man has ever given you. You're going to awake tomorrow and know that I'm the only man in your life from now on."

Her eyes fell to some point in the centre of his chest. "You've already given me one rose," she reminded him. She put her head on one side, feeling a little braver. "Is Thanksgiving sometime soon? We don't have it over here."

"It's a big family occasion with us. Everybody goes home for Thanksgiving in the States." He smiled a wry smile. "Mary Beth will be expecting you to join us anyway. It's on the last Thursday in November."

"Oh, quite near Christmas. Isn't that a bit much, eating turkey with all the trimmings in November and again a month later?"

But he wouldn't hear anything against the American custom and, once he had finished explaining its significance to her, she began to think it was a good idea also. Perhaps one day she would go to the American Boston and see where he lived; they would make their own Thanksgiving there. It was only a dream, but dreams didn't hurt anyone except the dreamer.

While he was talking, recalling the various happy festivals he had enjoyed as a child, Sarah looked round the kitchen. She hoped James had got in a good supply of soap. Noting that the greasy grime got worse as one went higher, she realized that she was going to get off with a much lighter task than his.

"Hadn't we better get started?" she suggested at last. She leaned against the Welsh dresser that had taken her eye from the first moment she had walked into the kitchen, and bent down to open the cupboards to see what was inside. "This is a gorgeous piece! Look at it! Made from solid oak!"

"You wouldn't rather have a built-in kitchen with all the latest gadgets?"

Sarah shook her head. "I wouldn't change a thing! It would be a positive pleasure to scrub that table, and the chairs are works of art! One could sit on them all day and be comfortable. I hate those modern ones with spindly legs, that have a totally different shape from mine—or, worse still, those high stools that I can never get up on."

"Okay, you've convinced me. I'll get a new cooker and leave it at that."

"And a new sink," she added firmly, having seen the spiders that had settled in the one that was already there, a monstrous structure made from what looked like painted concrete.

"Right. What are we going to do for lunch meanwhile?"

She turned, laughing at him. "Thinking of your stomach already? We'll go to the local pub and you can sample our local beer—"

He came towards her, looping his arms about her. "And what will you have?"

She gave it some thought, still laughing. "I don't care for beer," she confessed. "I'll probably have a fruit juice, or if I'm cold by that time I'll have a double whiskey and hang the consequences!"

"That's something I'd like to see!" he said. He kissed her on the tip of her nose and she thought how nice he was, and how much in love with him she was, and how she wished he would woo her with an armful of roses after all.

She said, "You probably will if we stand about here much longer. It isn't very warm, is it?"

They made a good start at getting the walls ready for the paint he had bought. Sarah was by far the more experienced home decorator, a fact in which she took such obvious satisfaction. He spent a lot of time sitting on one of the wooden kitchen chairs and watching her as she showed him how it was to be done.

"I hadn't realised Americans were such lazy lumps!" she said after a while, frowning down at him from the top of a stepladder. "All those loose bits have to come off and the cracks filled in. I'm not going to do it all!"

"You're doing quite a good job," he said.

"Single-handed!" she berated him.

"I like watching you. It's remarkable that anyone so graceful can be so efficient."

"Well, I don't like spiders! You'll have to cope with them!" she insisted.

"Yes, ma'am."

By lunchtime the kitchen was looking very different. Worse, Sarah thought, but then places usually did before the paint went on. She stood in the middle of the room, checking their progress with a frowning concentration that amused her companion.

"What now?" he asked her.

She brushed her hands together, wincing as she felt their roughness. "I'll get cleaned up and then you can take me for lunch." She tried to move past him, expecting him to move out of her way, but he stood still, staring at her as though he had never seen her before. "Have I got a smut on my nose?" she teased him.

She felt her own muscles tighten up expectantly and she couldn't have moved if he'd paid her. She licked her lips, swallowing the lump in her throat, her eyes wide and a little scared by the strength of her own emotions.

"Damnation!" he swore, quite distinctly and, as if it were a coded signal, the tension tightened another notch until she felt she couldn't bear it another instant. Something would explode inside her and she would never be the same again.

"James." It was almost a question, though she hadn't intended it as such.

"Damnation," he said again. "I want you so badly, Sarah darling."

"I want you too."

He pulled her close up against him, holding her tightly in an embrace neither of them wanted to end.

"I suppose you do want lunch?" he whispered in her ear.

Was this the time to tell him she'd never been here before? Sarah screwed up her courage to the sticking point and then changed her mind again. She didn't know what his reaction would be, but she suspected it would be explosive. He might even take it into his head to take her back to Boston. She wanted to be with him, no matter what the cost; she wanted to be with him, close to him, closer than to anyone else in the world.

"If we don't have lunch, we won't finish preparing the kitchen today. And if we don't paint it tomorrow,

I won't be able to cook Sunday lunch here, and I thought—I thought that would be homey and—and comfortable."

He relaxed a trifle. "What are you planning to cook?"

"Roast beef and all the trimmings—if I can get that stove to work."

"We'll have the new one in by then," he promised. "I'll see about it this afternoon. You'll have to give me a list of everything you need."

Sarah thought he had a lot to learn about the vagaries of deliveries in the country, but she thought it better to hold her peace and let him find out for himself.

"There has to be a village shop somewhere about. I'll be able to buy all I need there. The cooker and the sink I'll leave to you."

She was glad that he didn't attempt to follow her when she went upstairs to change her clothes again. She gave herself a long, hard look in the mirror and decided that whatever happened she wasn't going home.

"Sarah Gilbert," she told herself, "if you turn back now you'll regret it all your life."

It was a pleasant walk into the village. It led by the side of one of the black fields of the fens, past a water mill where they advertised for sale the flour they stone-ground there every Saturday, and into what passed for the main street, where there was more than one shop, a pretty little church and vicarage, and a pub called the Royal Oak, despite being a long way away from the original tree where Charles II was reputed to have hidden from Cromwell's armies when he made his escape to France. The whole village was built in the white, creamy stone that graces Cambridgeshire. It looked very pretty, with the last of the flowers of the year gracing the gardens, and the vegetable patches newly dug and ready for seeding for next year's crop.

The pub was comfortably full, with a great crackling fire in an inglenook at one end of the saloon.

"Have you ever played darts?" Sarah asked James.

"Never."

The landlord gave James a knowing look. "'Tain't a lady's game," he said. "Don't you go letting her beat you, and don't go letting her tell you the rules neither. Arthur'll do that!"

Sarah said, "Just as well, because I've never played before either. What do we have to do?"

The man called Arthur removed his flat cap and put it back on at a more jaunty angle. He picked up three darts and started to tell James where he should stand and how to throw them at the board for the best results. Sarah he ignored altogether.

"I'll get the drinks," she offered.

"Mine's a bitter," Arthur volunteered.

James would have abandoned the game to come and help her, but Arthur was launched on his explanation of the intricate scoring and had no intention of letting him go.

Sarah ordered a lager for James, a pint of bitter for Arthur, and a dry sherry for herself. The game was hotting up behind her, with Arthur getting more of a game than he'd bargained for.

"Don't get many of them in here nowadays," the landlord vouchsafed as she handed over a five-pound note to pay for the drinks.

"Many of what?"

"Yanks. Nice folk usually. What's he doing here?"

"He's bought a house in the village," Sarah explained. She went on to tell him which one and listened with interest to a resumé of the house's recent history.

"Are you going to live in it with him?" the landlord asked. "Take some doing up, that will."

"I'm the hired help," Sarah told him solemnly. "We started on the kitchen this morning. We can't actually cook anything in it yet, though. Is there any possibility of our having something to eat here?"

"Do you some sandwiches with a homemade soup, if that's your fancy?"

Sarah said that would do very well and took her drink over to a chair by the fire, from where she could watch James without being observed herself. It amused her that he should bring the same fierce concentration to a game of darts that he did to everything else. His hair was ruffled from where he had run exasperated fingers through it, but he was getting the hang of it now; she could tell by the triumphant smile that pulled at the corners of his mouth. James didn't like to lose, she reflected. It was a trait that must make him a very good lawyer, but it might be uncomfortable in his personal life.

The door opened again and another couple came in. Sarah peered round the corner of the inglenook to get a better look at them and was astonished to see that the man was Paul. The girl hanging on his arm and looking up at him with a worshipping expression was someone she knew well from their folksinging sessions, Susan Hardwick. Susan, who couldn't sing but didn't know it, and who hated dancing quite as much as Paul did. What a happy coincidence, Sarah thought, that they should have got together. She stood up with a warm smile and went forward to greet them.

Chapter Ten

Sarah hoped it was only she who had noticed how Susan's face fell at the sight of her. It had been the same story all along, she thought, and she wondered how she could have been so blind. Susan sang, but Sarah sang better and was the one who was always asked to front their strictly amateur efforts at songwriting and performance. Susan had wanted to attract Paul; Sarah hadn't cared one way or the other but had nevertheless succeeded in keeping his attention on herself for far too long.

"Hullo, Susan; hullo, Paul!"

James turned his head at the name, glaring at the newcomers. He flung the last of his darts blindly at the board and strode over to cut Sarah off from offering her cheek to Paul's shamefaced greeting.

"How lovely you have Susan with you!" Sarah said loudly and entirely for James's benefit.

Paul looked more uncomfortable still. "I didn't think you'd mind," he began. "What are you doing here?"

Sarah smiled ruefully at herself. Here goes, she thought, here is where I burn my boat once and for all. It would be all over Boston by morning, but so what? She was proud to be with James Foxe.

"I'm staying the weekend with James," she said, and her voice hardly quivered at all. "He's bought a house in the village . . ."

Susan's eyes were as round as saucers. "You're here alone with James?"

"For the weekend," Sarah confirmed.

Paul gave her a bleak look. "I hope you know what you're doing," he said stiffly. "You'll never be able to keep it quiet, you know."

"I shan't try," Sarah said. "I'm not ashamed of what I'm doing."

Paul was shocked, but Susan was a horrid mixture of the triumphant and the prurient. "People'll never believe me!" she gasped. "Not of Sarah! Who would have thought it?"

"You're well out of it," James informed Paul distantly. "Sarah'd run you ragged in a week. She needs a firm hand—"

"Do I, indeed?" Sarah interrupted him indignantly.

Once James was launched, however, he was very difficult to stop. "I'd try another pub, if I were you," he went on to Paul. "Your girl friend will feel more comfortable and so will mine."

Startled to hear herself referred to in such terms, Sarah made one last protest. "They may like to share our sandwiches," she said.

James glared at her. "They're not sharing anything of mine! I don't share—"

Sarah's temper, usually as placid as a dew pond on a calm day, flared. "Not even normal good manners! Paul and Susan are both friends of mine!"

James reached out a hand, grasping Sarah's arm so tightly she was sure she would have a bruise for days. "Susan may be a friend of yours, for all I know. Paul is an ex-friend. If he isn't going, I am!"

"We'll go," Paul agreed hastily. "We don't want any trouble."

Sarah waited until both Paul and Susan had gone, shutting the door carefully behind them. The situation between her and James was rapidly getting out of hand, and she didn't know what to do about it.

"That was unforgivable!" she bit out at James. "You have no reason to be jealous of Paul, and, even if you did have, my friends are my business. Don't ever make the mistake of trying to choose or dismiss one of them for me again!"

"You're still in love with Paul?"

"Don't be ridiculous! I never was in love with him, but I like him and I mean to go on having him as a friend. That is, if he still wants me as a friend. He must think me wanting not to have walked out of here with them!"

"Maybe it would have served me right, but I'm glad you didn't. I'm sorry, love. I see red whenever I trip over one of your old 'friends'; there seem to be so many of them. I want you to myself."

"Regardless of how I feel about it?"

His eyes glinted. "I know how you feel about it. You want me, too!"

Sarah gave him look for look. "I have my reservations about it," she told him. "I'm not one of your possessions!"

He grinned. "It sounds prickly, but I get the general idea."

"It's your attitude . . ." she began.

He sat down beside her in the inglenook. "There aren't many men who like the idea of sharing their women with another man."

She was shocked to the roots of her being. "But that's the whole point. I'm not your woman, am I?"

"Don't you want to be?"

"I've never been anyone else's," she said, so quietly that she wondered if he'd heard her. It was one of the most difficult things she had ever had to say.

"Don't suppose you see a fire like this often in America!" The landlord banged a plate of sandwiches down on the table in front of them. "'Ere's your grub! The soup's following as soon as the wife makes up her mind whether to put it in mugs or in proper plates like you'll be more used to. Been told all 'bout your fast food joints, as you call them. Terrible food, but set out nice, to make you think you're eating something special. Shouldn't care for it myself."

Sarah was hard put to it not to laugh. "Don't you ever have a hamburg and chips?" she asked him.

"French fries," he corrected her with a sniff. "I'll not say I don't, but only *English* hamburgs. Don't know what's in those foreign ones, do I? Could be cat food, for all I know."

James laughed as Sarah did, but he became very quiet after that. Sarah hoped the landlord hadn't offended him, though she didn't think so, for he was so obviously a character that no one could have taken him seriously. It was only when they were walking home that she realised he hadn't been listening to what the landlord had been saying at all.

"Are you still staying the weekend?" James asked her.

"Do I have a choice?"

He nodded slowly. "If I've been wrong about you, you'll probably choose to go—"

"I'm staying," she said.

He smiled, looking suddenly lighthearted. "Good." He didn't say anything more; he didn't have to. But Sarah thought they'd both learned something from the incident in the pub. She certainly had. She'd learned that no man, no matter how much you loved him, was perfect, any more than she was herself. James could be awkward, moody, and insanely possessive, but it hadn't made an atom of difference to how she felt about him.

It had been dark for a couple of hours when Sarah climbed down from the stepladder for the last time and surveyed her handiwork. The kitchen looked good. She had no idea how James had managed it, but he had tracked down a modern electric cooker and had succeeded in bringing it home with him, together with some instructions as to how it should be fitted.

"If you blow the fuse, don't expect me to mend it," she had warned him.

He had laughed up at her. "Not as handy as you like to pretend?"

"I have no experience of dealing with fuses," she had said with dignity.

His whole body had tensed. "Only men?"

She had sat on the top of the ladder, swinging her legs. "You'll find out," she had said. The thought had made her heart lurch painfully. What would he do when he did find out? she wondered.

She had tried to put the whole business out of her mind after that and had been successful, too. She had enjoyed the tea he had made her which had tasted of wet straw, and had asked him to remind her in future to choose coffee when he was fixing the drinks. Now there seemed to be nothing between her and bedtime and she still hadn't made up her mind how she was going to play the scene.

James looked round the kitchen with satisfaction. "All our own work," he said triumphantly. "We make a great team."

"I'm glad you think so," she had come back dryly. "If you had my aching muscles you'd know who'd done the greater part!"

He grinned at her. "Complaining again?"

"I'm hungry," she confessed, seizing on anything that would come between her and the intimate moments she knew lay ahead.

"Chinese take-away suit you? I got some when I picked up the cooker. Why don't you take a shower while I heat it up and try to light the fire in the sitting room?"

"Is there any hot water?" she demurred. There wouldn't be a shower in a house like this one, but there might be a bath—if she cleaned it first.

"There'd better be! I paid a monstrous fee to the electricity company to have it reconnected last week, and the lights seem to be working."

Sarah took herself off upstairs before he changed his mind, glad of a few moments by herself to get herself in hand. The bath was old-fashioned and stood on four ornamental legs. She ran the hot water into it and it gushed out of the taps in a cloud of steam that was reassuring. Prowling through the toiletries that someone—James?—had put out on the shelf over the basin, she came across some rose-scented bath cubes and dropped two of them into the hot water with calculated extravagance. That took care of the bath, she thought. The next problem was what she was going to wear afterwards.

Her dressing gown was an old cast-off of her mother's. It was made of a silky man-made fabric and had a wide sash that was more glamourous than anything else she had with her. Despite the warmth she had gained from the bath, Sarah was shivering as she made her way downstairs to where James was waiting for her. Outside the sitting room, she swallowed hard to give herself courage. She even raised her hand to knock on the door before she realised what she was doing. She could smell the sweet-and-sour pork hotting up in the kitchen and wondered why she had thought she would ever be hungry again. What she was, was paralysed with fear! She had never thought of herself as the heroine of an affair, but as a woman with a husband who loved her and whom she loved in return.

"Did that get rid of the aches and pains?" James asked her as she pushed open the door and went inside.

"Yes." She obeyed the summons of his hand and

went and sat beside him on the hearth rug in front of the now blazing fire. "Thank you."

He surveyed her with satisfaction, lingering so long over the process that her cheeks were hot with a shyness she despised by the time he turned away. It was idle, no doubt, to hope he hadn't noticed and drawn his own conclusions. She put up a hand and released her long hair in a flood down her back. It gave her the opportunity to flick it forward, over her shoulders, so that she could hide behind it.

"You're very beautiful," he said at last.

"Thank you," Sarah said. She was embarrassed to look at him.

"The first time I saw you I knew you were the girl for me," he went on abruptly.

She looked at him then, her mouth open in astonishment. "No, don't say anything. I know you were too busy with your other friends for me to register with you, but you're here now, with me, and you're even more beautiful than I thought you were then. I'm a lucky man!"

"With Chinese take-away for dinner?"

She still wasn't looking at him. His words had touched some chord within her, arousing a painful need that was exciting even while she was half-scared by its intensity. She wondered if she had made a mistake in coming downstairs in her nightgown instead of getting dressed again. She would have felt less vulnerable fully clothed.

"Are you laughing at me?" he demanded.

Laughter was so far from her thoughts that she could only stare at him, noting for the first time that he was as tense and awkward as she. Did he really care what she thought of him? She had a power of her own and one that she relished. If he cared, really cared, that was everything she wanted from him.

"I wouldn't dare," she said.

He reached out a hand and pulled her down beside him, leaning up on his elbow so that he could watch her face in the firelight.

"Oh, yes you would!" He untied the sash of her mother's gown and pushed the garment away from her. "Can you wait a while for dinner?"

She nodded silently. She closed her eyes as he bent his head and took her mouth with his own, flicking his tongue against her lips until she caught up with the rules of the game and made him more welcome. His hands explored the soft curves of her flesh with a delight that was mutual. She reached up and pulled him closer to her, gasping a little as she felt his need for her and realised she had yet to convince him that this was the first time for her, that no other man had ever been allowed in her bed.

She was drowning in a sensuous lethargy that only he seemed able to command. Soon it would be too late; then she thought, I don't care, I'm where I want to be, why should I spoil it all now?

"James, I think you should know our dinner's burning!"

A gusty sigh was followed by the information that he was going to bring in their food. "I got a bit of everything. Will that do you?"

She nodded her head. She supposed she ought to help him, but she could no more have stood up than flown.

The draught from the open door made her shiver and she slipped her arms back into her gown, tying it tightly round the waist. Behind her, she could hear James's footsteps in the kitchen, and she rested her head on her knees.

She heard the pop of a wine cork coming out of the bottle and, a moment later, he was back, holding out a glass of champagne to her. She tried a sip, knowing it was bound to be a very good brand, and liked it. The only other time she had ever had champagne had been at her mother's wedding to her stepfather, and that hadn't tasted anything like this.

"Is it ruined?" she asked him, her voice breaking dangerously.

"No. You've half-killed me, but you've saved our dinner."

"I'm sorry," she said.

He touched her hair where the firelight was giving the illusion of a halo. "Suppose you tell me why," he suggested more gently. "There's no point in making yourself miserable over it."

"No," she agreed.

"Does champagne make you cry?"

"I don't know."

His eyes narrowed as he squatted down beside her. "Then suppose you tell me what's wrong and we can go on from there?"

"I'm trying to!"

"I'll get the food."

She had emptied her glass by the time he came back bearing two plates laden with a mixture of special fried rice, sweet-and-sour pork, barbecued spareribs, and chicken and almonds, together with a few prawns and a pile of bean shoots mixed up with something else.

"You'll feel better when you get this inside you," he said. "More wine?"

She held out her glass. "I feel better now."

"That's the champagne talking," he remarked wryly.

She made a face. "Dutch courage?"

"A little borrowed courage won't do you any harm. I have a feeling I'm beginning to know what you're going to tell me."

"I thought you'd be angry," she marveled. "I'm not promiscuous, not usually. I've never—I wanted to come with you! I love your house! I'm afraid I won't please you, but if you teach me what to do . . . James?"

"God," he groaned, "what have I done to you?"

"I want you to make love to me," she insisted stubbornly. "I wouldn't have come with you if I hadn't wanted that."

He began to eat. "Will a weekend be enough for you?"

Her mouth trembled. "I'd hoped for more," she admitted. "If you're going to be in Europe for a whole year, I thought—"

"And what about afterwards?"

She took a deep breath. "I don't want to think about that!" She sniffed. She wiped her nose on the back of her hand like a child and pushed her plate away from her. "I don't think I'm hungry after all."

He was unsympathetic. "Eat up!" he commanded her. "You're going to need all your strength in the next few days."

She didn't want to ask him what for. Besides, she thought she knew. He might have changed his mind about taking her as his mistress, but there was still the decorating to be done. She was good at that. She'd done a splendid job in the kitchen and it hadn't cost him a penny. It served her right, after the remarks she had made about the way Americans spent their dollars.

She did eat and, after a while, she began to enjoy what she was eating, though she enjoyed the champagne more.

"I could drink champagne every day," she said, as he filled her glass for the third time.

"Not at this price, you won't!"

She toasted him silently. "Is it very expensive? It must be a very good marque. It doesn't taste a bit like the stuff we had at Mother's wedding."

His smile was full of self-mockery. "And to think I thought you a sophisticated young woman who'd tried everything there was to try!"

"That was Jenny. I told you I'm not at all like Jenny."

"So you did." The affectionate look in his eyes made her blink. She was probably imagining it, or it might be the champagne that was producing the warm glow inside her. Perhaps she'd better not drink any more.

"Well, I'm not, am I?" she insisted, rolling the liquid round her glass and watching the spiral of bubbles rise to the surface.

"Not a bit," he agreed.

"So that's all right. I don't like Jenny."

"She had her points," he said.

Sarah frowned. "I don't want to hear about her. She made you unhappy—"

"And that matters to you?"

She nodded solemnly. "I don't like Jenny," she repeated stubbornly.

James peeled a king prawn and popped it into her mouth. "I'd better make some coffee before you go and get dressed," he said. "That champagne is going to your head."

"It's a lovely feeling!" Her frown deepened. "Why don't we go to bed after we've had our coffee?"

"Because," he answered sternly, "I'm not at all sure you know what you're doing and I've never yet taken advantage of an innocent young woman, high on champagne. Good Lord, Sarah, I wouldn't have brought you here at all if I'd known!"

She wriggled her toes. "I wish I hadn't told you!" she muttered.

"It's just as well for you you did!" he retorted sharply. He went back into the kitchen and she could smell the coffee percolating. "I'd probably have taken a stick to you if you hadn't," he called out from the doorway.

She thought that funny, not believing a word of it. "It's very lowering not to be taken seriously," she told him.

He came back with the coffee. "Oh, I take you seriously; just how seriously you'll find out. Now, drink this up and then I'm going to take you home."

"To Boston?" she exclaimed in dismay.

"To your mother's."

Sarah shook her head until her hair was whirling

about her shoulders. "She's not expecting me. Besides, she won't like it if we sleep in the same room under her roof. She's old-fashioned, and it wouldn't be good manners. We'd do far better to stay here."

James took a firm hold on the nape of her neck, turning her face to his. "I'm old-fashioned, too!" he growled. He looked deep into her eyes for a long moment and then he kissed her, a long, passionate kiss that sobered her up more than any amount of coffee would have done.

"Please, James, make love to me," she pleaded with him when he at last released her.

"Sarah, my love, don't argue with me tonight. I've done you enough damage without seducing you with French champagne at twenty pounds a bottle!"

"What's that got to do with anything?" she demanded.

"It means I'm not going to buy you for thirty dollars. I'll have you as a free gift, or not at all! Will you go and get dressed now?"

Sarah couldn't get her mind to work properly all the time she was changing. A free gift didn't sound as if he was never going to see her again. Perhaps the next time she'd manage things better and he wouldn't feel guilty about her lack of experience. After all, why should he care? He hadn't liked it when he'd thought she was bedding down with half the neighbourhood either.

He had the car started when she went downstairs again.

"You don't have to be in such a hurry to get rid of me," she complained as she got in beside him.

He took her bag and threw it onto the back seat. "Darling Sarah," he said very slowly, "that's the last thing I'm trying to do. Think about it, and you'll see what I mean. I'll see you tomorrow and we'll sort it all out then, okay?"

She nodded, because there didn't seem to be anything else to do. "All right," she said.

Chapter Eleven

Mrs. Bourne was a long time coming to the door. When she answered it, Sarah saw that she was already ready for bed, but one glance at her daughter's white face was enough for Sarah to be hurried inside, an arm protectively about her.

"Are you coming in too?" Mrs. Bourne asked James.

He looked very big and powerful as he stood on the doorstep. Sarah took a step closer to her mother and felt an answering squeeze on her arm.

James said, "I'll be back in the morning. Look after her for me, won't you? Will it be too early for you if I come to breakfast?"

"I think we can manage that," Mrs. Bourne answered thoughtfully. "Shall we say nine o'clock?"

"I'll be here," James promised.

Mrs. Bourne shut the door after him with an even

more thoughtful look on her face. "Have you two quarrelled?" she asked Sarah.

"Not exactly."

"How, not exactly."

Sarah gave her a despairing glance. "You wouldn't understand!"

"Try me," her mother invited. "We'll go into the kitchen and I'll make you a mug of something hot. You look as though you could do with it."

"I've been drinking champagne," Sarah told her. "Is it true that one doesn't get a hangover if one sticks to champagne?"

"I've never had the opportunity to try it out. What were you celebrating?"

Sarah wondered how to answer that. She was still wondering when she sat down at the kitchen table and watched as her mother put the kettle on.

"Try the truth," Mrs. Bourne advised dryly. "You never were much of a liar, and you'll only make bad worse if you tell me some fairy story that I won't believe anyway."

"You're right," said Sarah. "James has bought a cottage—"

"And you were going to spend the weekend with him there?"

Sarah looked at her mother with a new respect. "How did you guess?" Her mother had sounded quite normal, as if she were discussing the weather rather than her daughter's succumbing to a fate worse than death.

"It wasn't very difficult. You were more than half in love with James when you were here the other weekend. Did you change your mind, or did he?"

"He did. Apparently he doesn't seduce innocent young women, high on champagne. He thought I'd had experience, you see, and when I told him I hadn't, that was that! He told me to get dressed and he brought me here."

"And how did you feel about that?"

"I was disappointed."

Her mother plonked a mug of hot chocolate down in front of her, trying not to laugh. "You ought to be flattered. I don't suppose James has ever done the noble thing around any girl before. He must care about you."

Sarah heaved a sigh. "I wish I thought so. I think he was just feeling guilty." And she went on to tell her mother about the felling of Richard and how he had almost come to blows with Paul as well. "He walked out on me once because he thought I was like Jenny."

"Jenny?"

"He was going to marry Jenny, but she married someone else."

"More fool her!"

"That's what I thought," Sarah agreed. "Mary Beth thought he might be upset about it, that that was why he'd agreed to work at the International Court at The Hague for a while, but I don't think he loved her, really loved her at all! He says she had her points and would have made a suitable wife for an ambitious lawyer. She doesn't sound at all nice!"

"And he thought you were like her?"

Sarah nodded. "He thought I'd play around behind his back too."

Her mother's look of astonishment made Sarah feel

considerably better. She could almost laugh about it herself now.

"But he couldn't stay away from you?" Mrs. Bourne murmured. "Doesn't that tell you something?"

Sarah blew on her chocolate. "I thought so this morning. He came bursting in to my flat, demanding I cancel all my engagements and go off with him for the weekend so that he could prove to me that if I had him I wouldn't need anyone else. You'd love his cottage! We spent the day doing up the kitchen—"

"And you went along with this?"

"Yes," Sarah said simply. "I wanted to go with him."

Mrs. Bourne favoured her daughter with a long, level look. "He may not have marriage in mind, Sarah love," she pointed out gently.

"I know. I don't care. I still want to be with him. I know he'll go back to America eventually, but anything might have happened by then. If I can't have James, I don't think I shall ever want anyone else."

"You're in love with him," Betty Bourne observed. "You could get hurt."

But Sarah shook her head. "I don't think so. He brought me here, didn't he?"

"True, but you still don't know what he has in mind—"

Sarah's green eyes sparkled with a determination her mother had never seen before. "I know what *I* have in mind," Sarah said. "I promised him I'd cook the Sunday lunch for the two of us on his new stove and I mean to do just that, no matter what he has to say tomorrow." She gave a brisk little nod to her head. "He won't know what's hit him by the time I've finished with him. Isn't that what you'd do?"

Her mother laughed. "Probably, but I believe in man management. You never have."

"I've never had cause to before," Sarah said. "James is cause enough for anyone! You do like him, don't you?" she added somewhat uncertainly.

"Very much," Mrs. Bourne hastened to assure her. "If I didn't have David, I'd be quite envious. Did you bring some night things with you, or shall I lend you some of mine?"

Sarah let the doorbell ring twice before she went to answer it. She turned the gas down under the sausages, wiped her hands on her apron, and danced into the hall, a bright smile on her face.

He was ringing the bell for the third time when she wrenched it open and stood back to allow him to come in. Her eyes widened as she took in the picture he presented, his arms filled with long-stemmed red roses by the dozens, each one as perfect as the one next to it.

"For me?" The words came out in an awed whisper, quite different from the assured self she had meant him to find that morning. "James! Where on earth did you get them at this hour of the morning?"

"With difficulty." He grinned at her. "I know, I know, don't tell me, first the champagne and now six dozen red roses! If I want to spend my hard-earned dollars on you, my darling, you'll have to learn to put up with it. I'm only just getting into my stride."

"I'm overcome," Sarah said.

"Good. Stay that way! Am I allowed to come inside?"

"Oh yes, of course," she answered vaguely, holding the door wide. She eyed him uncertainly. "Are you trying to bribe me?" she asked.

He dropped a kiss on the end of her nose. "I'm wooing you, Miss Sarah Gilbert, and that's a different thing altogether."

"But I don't want to be wooed," she wailed. "I want to be won!"

"Patience, sweetheart, I have something to prove to you first."

"What?" she demanded suspiciously.

He shut the door for her, piling the roses into her arms. "I don't think this is the right time or place for that sort of conversation. After breakfast, we'll drive back to the house and we'll be alone there all day. We can talk then."

"And tonight?"

His teeth snapped shut a bare inch from her nose. "Let's live through today first, shall we?"

It didn't seem to Sarah that she was going to have much choice in the matter. She led the way to the kitchen, dropping the roses into the sink and turning on the tap. She had long ago found out that nothing revives flowers or keeps them going longer than giving them a good start and burying them in water up to their heads for half an hour or so.

"Good gracious!" Sarah's mother exclaimed as she came in and saw what her daughter was doing. "Are you going to leave some of those behind, by any chance?"

"No, I'm not. They're part of James's wooing and, as it doesn't look as though I'm going to get anything better than roses and champagne in the next few days, I'm hanging on to them."

"Sarah!"

A chuckle escaped James's iron control. "Pay no attention to her, Betty," he advised. "She's sore because she thought she'd taught me better than to throw my dollars around, impressing the natives."

Mrs. Bourne limped over to the nearest chair. "Sarah!" she exclaimed a second time.

"He conned me into thinking him a tightwad," her daughter retorted, not at all put out. "I thought he was going to treat me as an equal, leaving me to live in the slum of my choice and to pay my own way. It hasn't been like that at all. First, my car was too small, then I had to work my fingers to the bone transforming familiar squalor into something fit for a princess, and now it's roses and champagne. Where will it all end, I ask myself?"

"If you don't know, I'm leaving it to James to tell you," Mrs. Bourne said firmly. "Eat your breakfast and then clear out, both of you! I promised David we'd be on our own this weekend and I mean to keep my promise. He was called out to a horse last night and he only got back an hour or two ago and he'll think he has to get up before he's ready to if he hears you chattering about the place."

Sarah smiled a knowing smile at her mother across the table. "May I take a joint out of the freezer? There isn't much at the cottage."

"Take whatever you want, except the turkey. That's for Christmas."

It was a highly enjoyable breakfast. Sarah cooked sausages, bacon and eggs, and some rather green tomatoes from the garden, and worried if it was the kind of thing James liked. He ate everything that was put in front of him, however, and even had a second cup of her mother's coffee.

"That was good!" he said when he'd finished.

"You wouldn't rather have had pancakes, or waffles?"

He shook his head. "I like your English sausages."

"The coffee—"

He smiled out of the corner of his mouth. "One of these days I'll teach you how to make coffee the good old American way. Meanwhile, that was the best I've had over here."

Mrs. Bourne took herself off shortly after that to see if her husband was awake yet. She kissed both Sarah and James impartially, bidding them look after themselves, and left them alone together.

"I like your mother," James said. "Did she give you some good advice last night?"

"Mmm," said Sarah. "She said you must care about me or you wouldn't have brought me to her. True?"

"What do you think?"

"I think, next time, we'll leave out the champagne, and then I'll have a better chance to have my way with you."

James's eyes sparkled beneath creased brows. "It's remarks like that, my girl, that led me to believe you knew what you were doing with men. Now that I know you better—"

"You don't know me at all!"

"I know I can put you in a dither any time I choose, my love, and that you're not at all like Jenny."

She cast him a speaking look, not quite knowing how to answer. It was better for the moment, she thought, to take refuge in her mother's deep-freeze and choose what they'd need for the weekend. She took out an expensive cut of beef and a leg of lamb, noting the prices so that she could repay her parents later on. Then she filled up the plastic bag with a variety of vegetables and a packet of crêpes suzette which she hadn't seen before, but thought was worth a try as it was put up by a very reliable firm.

"Right, I'm ready," she said at last.

He took the supplies from her and carried them out to the car. Sarah followed more slowly, her overnight bag dangling from her hand and the roses clasped in the crook of her arm. It bothered her that he knew she wasn't half as confident as she pretended to be. She'd thought she could put on an act that would dazzle him into declaring himself once and for all. Now she wasn't so sure.

"Which room are we going to tackle today?" she asked as she got into the car.

"I've got something better for us to do today."

That sounded better. She threw him a look of mute enquiry, but he refused to answer. He was smiling to himself in the most maddening way. Sarah turned her head away and looked out at the passing scenery with determination. She could have done without guessing games so early in the morning.

"We're not going to the cottage!" she realised. "Where are we going?"

"We're going into Cambridge first."

"Oh." It wasn't what she wanted to do. She thought about trying to dissuade him, but one look at his face was enough to convince her that he wasn't in the mood to listen. So much for her attempts at man management, she told herself ruefully. It wasn't he who was being managed; it was she, with a skillful charm that left her breathless. "Why?" She hoped she didn't sound as sulky as she felt.

"It's all right, you won't have to get out of the car if you don't want to. I have to pick up something, and then we'll be going back to the cottage."

The car park was a depressing place, but as James had done nothing to encourage her to go with him, saying he'd be much quicker on his own, Sarah possessed herself in patience as well as she could, refusing to give way to the unaccountable depression that gripped her.

He was back almost immediately. "What did you get?" she asked him.

"Something I'll want to have by me later if I get the right answers first."

She couldn't make head nor tail of what he was talking about, nor did she feel he would welcome being questioned any further.

"I hope there are some vases at the cottage," she said instead. "We'll have roses everywhere."

The cottage was much as she had left it. James had raked out the old fire, and laid a new one which he lit as soon as they got in. Sarah stood and watched him, feeling like the fifth wheel on the coach as he held a newspaper up in front of the grate and was rewarded by a mighty roar of flame that soon lit the kindling and was coaxed into a warming fire.

"What can I do?" she asked shyly.

"I thought you were busy with the roses and putting the supplies away."

"Yes, I am," she said, more uncertain than ever.

It took some time to find enough receptacles to hold all the roses. She took the best of the arrangements into the sitting room, carrying the rest of them upstairs and into the bedroom. She put them on the dressing table and sat on the end of the bed, admiring them for a while.

By the time she went downstairs she had pulled herself together. She had redone her hair and her makeup and knew she was looking her very best. James had pushed the elderly, comfortable sofa up close to the fire and he stood up at her appearance, beckoning her to sit beside him, with a great fluffy cushion behind her back.

He took her hand in his. "Am I forgiven?"

She blinked. "It depends what for."

"For being a possessive idiot who wants you all to himself."

She said, "Oh, that!"

"Well?"

"I like my friends, but that's all they are, James, all they've ever been to me."

"I know that now. I'll try to remember it in the future. I'd make you a promise, but I'm not sure I'd keep it. I've never felt about anyone the way I feel about you, Sarah Gilbert, and I burn up inside when I see you smiling at another man."

She felt very wise and much older than her years. "You won't when you're sure of me," she said. "I'm like my mother in that, the faithful type. She never looked at another man all the time my father was alive and now it's just the same with David. Neither of them ever had any doubt they came first with her. I don't know why it should be so, but you come first with me."

He was silent for a long moment, then he said, "Marry me, Sarah?"

She turned wide green eyes onto him. "Isn't it a bit soon for that?" she asked. "You haven't known me long—"

"Long enough! Far too long not to have you in my arms and in my bed!"

She caught her breath. "You don't have to marry me for that," she said. "I'd rather have a willing lover than an unwilling husband. I'm not anything like Jenny. You don't have to bribe me to marry you."

"No, you're not like Jenny," he agreed. "You're nothing like her. Darling Sarah, don't you realise yet that if I don't marry you I'm going to regret it all my days. I can't live without you!"

"You haven't tried!"

"I have, after I thought you'd made that assignation with Richard. I've never been so miserable in my life. Even if I'd had to share you with half a dozen others, it'd be better than not having you at all. I love you!"

She rested her head against his shoulder as a warm, treacly feeling of relief seeped through her being. "I love you too," she said. "I wanted to go to Holland with you—"

He turned her face to his, effectively silencing her. She heaved another sigh of relief and gave herself up to the delights of his embrace, as eager to discover all there was to know about him as he was her.

It was a long time later when he took a small jeweller's box out of his pocket. "This is what we went to Cambridge to get." He opened the box to reveal the largest emerald Sarah had ever seen. "To go with the green of your eyes," he muttered. "Sarah, you will marry me, won't you?"

She nodded, rendered speechless for one of the few times in her life. He pressed the ring home onto her finger and bent to kiss her again.

"Say it, Sarah," he begged her. "Say it now!"

She licked dry lips, her heart swelling within her. "Yes, I'll marry you," she said softly. "I'll marry you because I can't live without you. You're life itself to me and I love you more than I can ever tell you."

He held her tight until she realised he hadn't been nearly as certain of her as he had pretended. "I love you," she said again.

"It's a good beginning," he approved, looking more his usual, confident self. He grinned suddenly. "In twenty, fifty years, you'll know what you're talking about. It's going to take me at least as long as that to get used to having you about. I'm really going to splurge my money over you!"

Sarah looked down her nose. "What about my career?" she demanded. "I've worked jolly hard to get that place on its feet."

He sat back against the cushions, moving her closer into his arms. "How about a branch office in Boston,

U.S.A.?" he suggested. "With a large staff to keep it ticking over when I want you to myself?"

"It's a deal," she said.

It was the first time they'd been back to the cottage since their marriage. Between whiles, they had snatched a quick visit to the American Boston, and Sarah had fallen in love with the States as quickly as she had fallen in love with her husband. Once or twice she had wondered what old St. Botolph, the saint who had given his name to the original town—Boston, St. Botolph's town—would have thought if he could have seen the daughter city, but then what would he have thought if he could have visited the far smaller market town of Boston in Lincolnshire?

They had been to Holland several times. Sarah had learned very little about her husband's work; she had been far too busy visiting the Dutch art galleries and getting to know the many paintings she had only seen before in reproduction. She was astonished to find a Rembrandt painting not dull and dingy at all, but bright with vibrant colours, having been recently cleaned. She had been shocked into really looking at the depicted scene and had been unable to talk about anything else for days.

But it was her marriage itself that had been the greatest revelation to her. It was such fun being James's wife. She couldn't remember a time when she had laughed so much or learned so many new things in such a short time, and not all of them to do with the marriage bed. James was passionate, possessive, and more than a little masterful at times, but it was the friendship he offered her that had been one of the best surprises in store for her. She had been in love with him from the beginning, but she liked him more and more each day. She had even teased him on one occasion that he was becoming her best friend as well as her husband.

"I mean to be everything to you," he had assured her, with a seriousness that had touched her deeply. "I want you to enjoy being with me more than anything else."

"So that I won't miss my other friends?" she had asked him, smiling.

He had laughed with her, readily admitting that it still riled him to see her in the company of another man, sure of her as he was. "It isn't that, though," he had told her. "It's because I feel only half alive when you're away from me."

It had been another moment to tuck away and treasure in her old age, she had thought, if only because that was the way she felt about him too.

The cottage had been completely redecorated while they'd been away. There was central heating, though the old fireplaces had been kept, as had some of the more comfortable pieces of furniture.

"Happy to be home?" he asked her as they sat, drowsing, in front of a roaring fire.

"I loved your Boston, though," she said as she nodded her head. "I hadn't realised how old and sleepy my Boston is nowadays. It was once one of the most important ports in the country, but nobody much goes there now."

"Except American tourists looking for their heritage!"

"Not forgetting the Australians," she reminded

him. There was a tart note in her voice for, since James had taken an interest in her small business and had put in a staff of his own choosing to man it on both sides of the Atlantic, it had taken off and was coining her in more money than she knew what to do with. "Are you going to open an office over there too?"

"Maybe, one of these days."

She opened green eyes. "Not now?"

"Definitely not now," he agreed. "I have other things on my mind right now."

She smiled a secret smile. "Tell me all," she invited him.

"Not until you've been upstairs and had a hot bath. I'll put the champagne on ice, and then, when you come back, I'll let down your hair and we can start where we left off once before."

"Sounds nice," she agreed. She was getting used to drinking champagne where she had once made do with a cup of tea or coffee.

"Then get going, woman!" He gave her a push in the right direction. "I'm impatient for the next bit!"

"The best bit?" she mocked him.

"It should be, the price I paid for the champagne!"

She got lightly to her feet, looking down at him and enjoying the view. "It wouldn't matter to me if there was no champagne," she found herself saying. "If you'd given me the time, I'd have done up the house for nothing, and I'd love it just as dearly—"

"I know. You're not like Jenny."

"You have more than enough ambition for both of us, but I think you ought to know I'll never be what your mother calls a corporate wife, or anything like it.

I don't want to push you further than you want to go.
If you get tired of making money and want to be poor
instead, that'll suit me just as well."

He rose also, a smile of genuine amusement kicking
up the corners of his mouth. "You're not still worrying because I choose to waste my substance buying
you roses—"

"And champagne, and first class travel, and
clothes—"

"I'm not buying you, sweetheart."

"I'm not for sale!"

He was still amused. "And here I was thinking that
all the genuine Puritans left for America."

"Don't tease me, James. It's important to me that
you should know you don't have to woo me any more.
I *want* to be with you. I like having things, but you
don't have to bribe me with goodies for the rest of our
lives."

He pulled her into his arms and she could feel his
laughter rumbling in his chest. She clenched her fists,
bringing them down hard on his shoulders. "I'm
serious, James! I want to give you something sometimes too!"

"Oh, you do, do you!" His hands on her back were
beginning to do their work of undermining her concentration on anything but him.

"What do I give you?" she demanded.

He pulled her closer still. He wasn't smiling now.
Instead there was an intent look in his eyes she had
learned to recognise as meaning that she had his full
attention.

"You give me yourself," he said.

She trembled with a familiar hunger to be closer

still to him. "Is that enough for you?" she asked huskily.

"It's the breath in my body, Sarah my love. I'll love and need you till the day I die."

Her fingers ran through his hair and she pulled his head down to hers, arching herself into his body for his kiss. She didn't deserve such happiness, she thought, but she was going to grasp what was offered to her with both hands.

"I love you, James," she said. "Please love me."

"All my life long," he promised.

It was a long time before they spoke again, and by then they were going upstairs, hand in hand to bed.

"What a waste of champagne," Sarah said, and wondered why he laughed.

Silhouette Romance

IT'S YOUR OWN SPECIAL TIME
Contemporary romances for today's women.
Each month, six very special love stories will be yours
from SILHOUETTE.

$1.75 each

☐ 100 Stanford	☐ 128 Hampson	☐ 157 Vitek	☐ 185 Hampson
☐ 101 Hardy	☐ 129 Converse	☐ 158 Reynolds	☐ 186 Howard
☐ 102 Hastings	☐ 130 Hardy	☐ 159 Tracy	☐ 187 Scott
☐ 103 Cork	☐ 131 Stanford	☐ 160 Hampson	☐ 188 Cork
☐ 104 Vitek	☐ 132 Wisdom	☐ 161 Trent	☐ 189 Stephens
☐ 105 Eden	☐ 133 Rowe	☐ 162 Ashby	☐ 190 Hampson
☐ 106 Dailey	☐ 134 Charles	☐ 163 Roberts	☐ 191 Browning
☐ 107 Bright	☐ 135 Logan	☐ 164 Browning	☐ 192 John
☐ 108 Hampson	☐ 136 Hampson	☐ 165 Young	☐ 193 Trent
☐ 109 Vernon	☐ 137 Hunter	☐ 166 Wisdom	☐ 194 Barry
☐ 110 Trent	☐ 138 Wilson	☐ 167 Hunter	☐ 195 Dailey
☐ 111 South	☐ 139 Vitek	☐ 168 Carr	☐ 196 Hampson
☐ 112 Stanford	☐ 140 Erskine	☐ 169 Scott	☐ 197 Summers
☐ 113 Browning	☐ 142 Browning	☐ 170 Ripy	☐ 198 Hunter
☐ 114 Michaels	☐ 143 Roberts	☐ 171 Hill	☐ 199 Roberts
☐ 115 John	☐ 144 Goforth	☐ 172 Browning	☐ 200 Lloyd
☐ 116 Lindley	☐ 145 Hope	☐ 173 Camp	☐ 201 Starr
☐ 117 Scott	☐ 146 Michaels	☐ 174 Sinclair	☐ 202 Hampson
☐ 118 Dailey	☐ 147 Hampson	☐ 175 Jarrett	☐ 203 Browning
☐ 119 Hampson	☐ 148 Cork	☐ 176 Vitek	☐ 204 Carroll
☐ 120 Carroll	☐ 149 Saunders	☐ 177 Dailey	☐ 205 Maxam
☐ 121 Langan	☐ 150 Major	☐ 178 Hampson	☐ 206 Manning
☐ 122 Scofield	☐ 151 Hampson	☐ 179 Beckman	☐ 207 Windham
☐ 123 Sinclair	☐ 152 Halston	☐ 180 Roberts	☐ 208 Halston
☐ 124 Beckman	☐ 153 Dailey	☐ 181 Terrill	☐ 209 LaDame
☐ 125 Bright	☐ 154 Beckman	☐ 182 Clay	☐ 210 Eden
☐ 126 St. George	☐ 155 Hampson	☐ 183 Stanley	☐ 211 Walters
☐ 127 Roberts	☐ 156 Sawyer	☐ 184 Hardy	☐ 212 Young

$1.95 each

☐ 213 Dailey	☐ 217 Vitek	☐ 221 Browning	☐ 225 St. George
☐ 214 Hampson	☐ 218 Hunter	☐ 222 Carroll	☐ 226 Hampson
☐ 215 Roberts	☐ 219 Cork	☐ 223 Summers	☐ 227 Beckman
☐ 216 Saunders	☐ 220 Hampson	☐ 224 Langan	☐ 228 King

Silhouette Romance

$1.95 each

☐ 229 Thornton	☐ 254 Palmer	☐ 279 Ashby	☐ 304 Cork
☐ 230 Stevens	☐ 255 Smith	☐ 280 Roberts	☐ 305 Browning
☐ 231 Dailey	☐ 256 Hampson	☐ 281 Lovan	☐ 306 Gordon
☐ 232 Hampson	☐ 257 Hunter	☐ 282 Halldorson	☐ 307 Wildman
☐ 233 Vernon	☐ 258 Ashby	☐ 283 Payne	☐ 308 Young
☐ 234 Smith	☐ 259 English	☐ 284 Young	☐ 309 Hardy
☐ 235 James	☐ 260 Martin	☐ 285 Gray	☐ 310 Hunter
☐ 236 Maxam	☐ 261 Saunders	☐ 286 Cork	☐ 311 Gray
☐ 237 Wilson	☐ 262 John	☐ 287 Joyce	☐ 312 Vernon
☐ 238 Cork	☐ 263 Wilson	☐ 288 Smith	☐ 313 Rainville
☐ 239 McKay	☐ 264 Vine	☐ 289 Saunders	☐ 314 Palmer
☐ 240 Hunter	☐ 265 Adams	☐ 290 Hunter	☐ 315 Smith
☐ 241 Wisdom	☐ 266 Trent	☐ 291 McKay	☐ 316 Macomber
☐ 242 Brooke	☐ 267 Chase	☐ 292 Browning	☐ 317 Langan
☐ 243 Saunders	☐ 268 Hunter	☐ 293 Morgan	☐ 318 Herrington
☐ 244 Sinclair	☐ 269 Smith	☐ 294 Cockcroft	☐ 319 Lloyd
☐ 245 Trent	☐ 270 Camp	☐ 295 Vernon	☐ 320 Brooke
☐ 246 Carroll	☐ 271 Allison	☐ 296 Paige	☐ 321 Glenn
☐ 247 Halldorson	☐ 272 Forrest	☐ 297 Young	☐ 322 Hunter
☐ 248 St. George	☐ 273 Beckman	☐ 298 Hunter	☐ 323 Browning
☐ 249 Scofield	☐ 274 Roberts	☐ 299 Roberts	☐ 324 Maxam
☐ 250 Hampson	☐ 275 Browning	☐ 300 Stephens	☐ 325 Smith
☐ 251 Wilson	☐ 276 Vernon	☐ 301 Palmer	☐ 326 Lovan
☐ 252 Roberts	☐ 277 Wilson	☐ 302 Smith	☐ 327 James
☐ 253 James	☐ 278 Hunter	☐ 303 Langan	

SILHOUETTE BOOKS, Department SB/1

1230 Avenue of the Americas
New York, NY 10020

Please send me the books I have checked above. I am enclosing $_____
(please add 75¢ to cover postage and handling. NYS and NYC residents please
add appropriate sales tax). Send check or money order—no cash or C.O.D.'s
please. Allow six weeks for delivery.

NAME _____

ADDRESS _____

CITY _____ STATE/ZIP _____

Silhouette Romance